Children of Stone

VINCENT MCDONNELL is from County Mayo and now lives near Newmarket, County Cork. In 1989 he won the GPA First Fiction Award, after being recommended by Graham Greene, and has since had seven novels for children published and two for adults. Many of his short stories have also been published and he has won numerous other prizes as well as being shortlisted for the RAI awards. He has been writer in residence at a variety of locations and has given workshops and readings all over Ireland.

Other children's titles by the same author

The Boy Who Saved Christmas
Race Against Time
Can Timmy Save Toyland?
The Knock Airport Mystery
Chill Factor
Out of the Flames

IN MEMORY OF MY FATHER

CHILDREN OF STONE

Vincent McDonnell

The Collins Press

Published in 2005 by
The Collins Press
West Link Park
Doughcloyne
Wilton
Cork

© Vincent McDonnell 2005
© Illustrations Deirdre O'Neill 2005

First published in 1994 by Poolbeg Press

Vincent McDonnell has asserted his moral right to be identified
as author of this work.

A Cataloguing-In-Publication data record for this book is available from the British Library

ISBN: 1-903464-88-9

Typesetting: The Collins Press

Font: Skia, 14 point

Cover design: Deirdre O'Neill

Printed in Ireland by Colour Books Ltd

1

PREPARATIONS FOR A JOURNEY

Ever so slowly the twilight closed in about the children. Soon it would be dark and they could leave to begin their perilous journey. But until then they could only wait and hope, and try to hide their fears.

Outside their stone-built house with its cone-shaped roof, the life of the village of Marn went on as usual. Bolan, the eldest of the children, crept to the window, a simple uncovered aperture in the wall, and stared out. He saw three labourers returning from the fields outside the palisade, weary after their day's work. In their aching and calloused hands, they carried their digging sticks.

Because it was summer and the weather was fine,

the chimney holes of the houses were closed up and the women were cooking outside. Fires were lighting, flickering tongues of flame in the gathering gloom. Mouth-watering smells of cooking meat mingled with the warm evening air. In the centre of the village, before the Assembly House, the children were playing. Bolan watched them, saddened that his brother couldn't join in. But all would return to normal once they were reunited with their father and he returned to the village.

Bolan turned away from the window and glanced at his younger sister and brother. They were huddled together in the corner of the room. Their frightened faces watched him, pale blurs in the gloom. He smiled to reassure them, and becoming aware that they couldn't see him properly, reached out a hand to ruffle his brother's thick dark hair.

'Do not be afraid, Vanu,' he said. 'I won't let anyone hurt you. Soon it'll be dark and we can leave. We'll have a great adventure travelling to Sarnay. In a few days we'll be with father and you can play again.'

The little boy did not speak. Instead, he stared at his brother, with his large eyes that looked like dark cavities in the white glow of his face. Despite the assurances, Vanu sensed the fear in his brother's voice and he edged still closer to Alna. Their mother had died when Vanu was born and Alna, now only ten, had taken her place.

Bolan continued to watch them. They were his responsibility now. Until they were reunited with their father, Gaelen, he would have to look after them. The enormous responsibility sat heavily on his twelve-year-old shoulders. The thought of the perilous journey which lay before them made the palms of his hands sticky with sweat.

Since Faver, his father's trusted advisor, came to warn him yesterday that Nevel was plotting to murder his father and take over leadership of the village, Bolan had lived with fear. Faver had told him Nevel would also kill Bolan himself, along with Alna and Vanu. He would not risk leaving any of them alive to one day wreak vengeance on him.

All through last night Bolan had lain awake trying to decide what he should do. To leave the village and follow their father to Sarnay, taking Alna and Vanu with him, seemed the height of folly. But he knew now that to remain would mean certain death for them all. He'd known they would die ever since the body of Faver was brought back to the village that morning.

Nevel had organised the hunt for wild boar that day, selecting Faver and five others to go with him. The five, who were allies of Nevel, had soon returned bringing the body of the dead Faver back with them.

3

They claimed he had fallen down a ravine but as the villagers gathered round the body they all knew Faver had been murdered. It was a warning to all of them. Anyone who opposed Nevel would die.

Bolan had stood at the edge of the group, aware of what the dead body signified for him and his family. If they remained in the village, Nevel would kill them. And if they didn't warn their father of the danger, he too would die as he made the return journey from Sarnay.

Sarnay was by the sea, a settlement built around the flint mines. It stood at the mouth of the river on which Marn itself was built. The traders who came from there, with their flint and bone tools, spoke of a long and hazardous journey. Bolan had often sat late into the night with the other villagers listening to the stories of the dangers to be encountered.

There were still nomads roaming the countryside, hunting and fishing. They were not to be trusted and it was said they would attack unwary travellers. Raiding parties often ventured out from Sarnay seeking slaves to work in the mines. Now too, raiding parties of fierce peoples from across the seas also came seeking slaves.

But these were not the only dangers to be encountered. The forests were teeming with animals. Ever-hungry wolves hunted in packs, showing no mercy.

There were wild boar which would attack a man, and the last of the great horned oxen which seemed to know no fear. But the most terrifying of all the animals was the bear who could cleave a man open from head to foot with one swipe of its great paw.

That was what faced the children if they ventured to travel. Even the traders who travelled in groups and who were well armed, sometimes showed fear when retelling their stories. But Bolan was aware that of the two choices facing him, to travel was the one offering the best hope. They could all die on the journey of course. But to remain in the village meant certain death.

He'd considered going alone, but dismissed it. How could he leave Alna and Vanu at the mercy of Nevel? He had promised his father to take care of them while he was away. When he went, they would have to come with him. It was a terrible responsibility to bear, but he was unlike other boys.

As the eldest son of the village's leader, Gaelan, he had been groomed from childhood to succeed his father. He'd been taught the skills of animal husbandry, knowledge of the land and the seasons. He could read terrain, the bent grass, the broken twigs, the wisp of hair caught on a bramble which indicated the passage of an animal or a human. He was an expert with a bow and arrow, could throw a spear with unerring accuracy, could prime a trap or catch a pike with the leister, a spear for catching fish made from barbed antler points. Of all the persons in the village who might be capable of undertaking such a perilous journey, Bolan would certainly be included in their number.

The darkness had thickened now so that when Bolan looked at his sister and brother they were like shadows. Soon they would leave. Bolan cocked his head and listened. Silence was descending on the village. Only a dog barked to break the stillness.

Bolan knew that once the people had eaten they would make their way to the Assembly House, where they would remain all night mourning Faver. It was part of their tradition and Nevel would not interfere with it. But Nevel might take advantage of the occasion to carry out his murderous intentions. Only he wouldn't do so until the mourning was well underway. That would not be for some hours yet. Bolan intended to be well away from the village by then though.

Everything had been prepared for the journey. Since he'd seen Faver's dead body lying in the dust by the east gate this afternoon, Bolan had feigned sickness. It had given him an excuse to remain at home all day. Here, he had been busy with Alna, making their preparations.

She had packed as much provisions as they could carry. Cooked meat and bread had been stowed away in pouches made of animal skin. She had packed wild honey, dried fruit and nuts which had been collected in the forest. The flints used for the lighting of fires were packed, along with some tinder. She also took a selection of herbs for medicinal purposes.

Bolan, meanwhile, had checked and re-checked his spear, bow and quiver of arrows. The flint arrowheads, brought to the village by the traders from Sarnay, were so sharp that a man could shave his beard with them. They were barbed to give a firm fitting in the shaft, and the feathers were dressed to ensure a true flight. Bolan could fell a deer with a single arrow, or kill a fleeing wild boar with his spear.

He had also selected various lengths of rope to take with him, along with a number of flint scrapers, a flint hand axe and the flint dagger his father had given him on his twelfth birthday. He now checked the antler grappling hook and ensured that the rope attached to it was firmly fixed. They would need the grappling hook to scale the palisade surrounding the village. They could not risk trying to leave by either of the two gates. It was almost certain that Nevel had them guarded now by his own men. They would have been given instructions to kill anyone trying to sneak out.

Bolan also checked his leister, for they would follow the course of the river which teemed with fish – trout, bony perch, pike and the eels which still wriggled while they cooked. The river would lead them south to the sea and to Sarnay. They would retrace their ancestor's footsteps, they who'd moved inland, away from the sea long years before. They had been nomads who had eventually settled here at Marn and became farmers when the original group grew too large for easy movement.

Under his grandfather's and then his father's rule, Marn had grown and prospered. They grew wheat, barley and oats, raised cattle, pigs, goats and sheep. But they still hunted for deer and wild boar. They fished the river in whose elbow the village was built and trapped smaller animals that roamed in the forest.

But then two dangers came to threaten them. Firstly, there were too many people in the village for the fields to support. Nevel wanted the village to be split. He would take half the people further inland and found another settlement with himself as leader. But Gaelan had opposed this. He knew Nevel only sought power for himself and did not have the interest of the people in mind.

Then traders who had come from Sarnay told of a new type of wheat called emmer. It had come from far-off lands across the sea and was said to give a much larger yield than the einkorn they now grew. This wheat would produce the extra food they needed to keep the village together. Gaelan's dream was to build a great settlement here, and one of his motives for travelling to Sarnay was to trade with the Lord there for this new grain.

Another reason for his travelling there was due to the second danger facing them. This came from the raiding parties from across the seas, those seemingly fearless and ruthless men who came seeking slaves and who were venturing further and further inland. They posed the greater threat to Marn and this was another reason put forward by Nevel for taking half of the village to a new settlement. Gaelan's solution to the problem, however, was to place the village of Marn under the protection of Sarnay.

Nevel opposed this plan, claiming that the tribute demanded by the Lord of Sarnay for his protection would be too great. But Gaelan had won the vote of the village council for his proposals and had undertaken the task of travelling to Sarnay. Faver had advised him not to go, insisting that Nevel would take the opportunity to seize control.

Gaelan had ignored the advice and now Faver was dead. If something was not done to stop Nevel and his cronies, then Marn was doomed.

Bolan was aware of all this as he moved again to the window aperture and looked out. Darkness had settled on the village and the fires were dying out. Light could be seen in the Assembly House, the largest building in the village. The villagers were gathering to mourn the death of Faver.

Bolan turned from the window.

'It is time,' he whispered to Alna and Vanu, though there was no one to hear. 'We must go now.'

He reached out a hand to touch his brother and the child trembled. Quickly Bolan withdrew his own hand, aware that he too was trembling.

1

THE PERILOUS JOURNEY BEGINS

Bolan crept to the entrance to the house and pulled aside the skin which was drawn across the opening. He stared at the Assembly House, alive with light and sound. Through the window apertures he could see the people inside. Elsewhere, the village was shrouded in darkness. The houses and other large buildings housing the threshing and granary shed and bakery seemed no more substantial than shadows.

Bolan averted his gaze from the Assembly House, letting his eyes become accustomed again to the darkness. There was no moon but the sky was sprinkled with stars. He found he could see for about 30 paces. It was enough. There was light to see by, yet darkness to hide them.

He returned to the room where Alna and Vanu waited. They did not speak but quickly and quietly gathered up their provisions. Even Vanu would have to carry his share. Alna took the grappling hook and leister while Bolan strapped on his quiver of arrows and thrust his arm through the bow so that it hung from his shoulder. His spear he grasped tightly in his hands, prepared to defend his sister and brother to the death.

Silently they crept to the entrance to the house. Here Bolan moved out into the open, aware that this was a terribly dangerous moment. If Nevel had someone watching the house, then all was lost. A shout would bring him and his men from the Assembly House. And Bolan knew he could not fight them all. He might kill some of them but they would easily overpower him. Then they would all die.

Bolan shivered but he knew it wasn't from the chill of the night air. Drawing in a deep breath he advanced further on the baked dry earth. But no warning shout came. He beckoned Alna and Vanu and they quickly joined him, moving as stealthily as he did. He hesitated for a moment, then led them off, away from the Assembly House. That was where the greater danger lay.

From house to house they moved like shadows, crouching by each wall and checking all around before venturing farther. Bolan had decided to scale the palisade on the southern side of the village. Then he would strike off into the forest until he reached the river. From there they would follow its course to Sarnay, keeping off the trail used by the traders.

Bolan had reckoned on having a few hours start at least. Indeed if luck was on their side, Nevel might not make a move until the next day. By then his men would be too drunk from their night of mourning to put up much of a chase. And even if Nevel discovered they had escaped in the next few hours, the men might be too frightened to venture into the forest at night. The years they had lived as farmers in the security of the palisade had made them fearful of what was outside. And with Faver dead, they would know his spirit was abroad tonight in the darkness.

This fear, coupled with the dangers of the forest, touched Bolan with icy tendrils. But he hid his terror, clenching his teeth. If Alna or Vanu sensed he was afraid, they too would become fearful. It was something his father had taught him on the hunt – some fear was a good thing. It was necessary. But too much paralysed a man. And a frightened man was a danger. He would always panic when called upon.

They crept on, keeping close to the houses until they reached the palisade itself. It loomed up before them,

13

more than twice the height of a man. It was built of oak logs, pointed at the top and sunk deep into the earth. It was buttressed with more oak logs, making it immensely secure. It was the ultimate protection for the village, both from animals and man.

The three children huddled at the foot of the barrier, relieved they had safely come this far. But until they scaled the palisade and melted into the forest, safety was only an illusion. Their eyes were accustomed to the darkness now and they stared at each other. Vanu shivered, as if cold, and Bolan touched his shoulder.

'We're going to climb the palisade now, Vanu,' he whispered. 'Once we're on the other side, the great adventure will begin. Are you ready?'

The little boy nodded.

'Good,' Bolan continued. 'Let's go then.'

With that, he handed his spear to Alna and took the grappling hook from her. Holding it in his right hand and the length of attached rope in the other, he moved to the foot of the nearest buttress. Taking aim, he threw the hook upwards into the darkness. The first attempt failed and the hook fell back to the ground. Bolan held his breath, listening for a warning shout. But none came.

He tried again and with his second attempt he was successful. The hook caught on the spiked top of a log. Bolan tugged on the rope but it held firm. He beckoned to the others and, gripping the rope, began to clamber up the buttress. Hand over hand he hauled himself upwards.

He reached the top of the palisade and saw the forest beyond, dark and seemingly impenetrable. He stared towards it, a lump rising in his throat. But there was no time to lose. Quickly he wedged himself between two of the spiked logs, ignoring the discomfort. He slipped his bow from his shoulder and hooked it on a nearby spike, leaving himself free for the task in hand.

Below him Alna had already tied two of the leather pouches to the end of the rope. Bolan now hauled them up and, after untying the knots, dropped them down on the other side on the string they had attached to them when they made their preparations. He hauled up a second lot and dealt with it in a similar manner.

It was with the third and final lot of their provisions that disaster struck. Alna had not tied the knots tightly enough and as Bolan reached for the large pouch, containing all of their meat, the knots gave way. The pouch plummeted down and struck Vanu on the shoulder, knocking him to the ground.

He wasn't hurt but the shock made him cry out.

His cry of terror echoed in the night air, seeming to soar above the village like a bird. Bolan held his breath, hoping no one had heard. For a second nothing happened and it seemed as if luck was on their side. But then a dog barked nearby and was immediately answered by others. Soon the whole village seemed alive with the barking and yelping which began to draw near. The dogs were coming straight towards them, becoming more excited and agitated as they caught the scent of fear emanating from the children.

It was Alna's quick thinking that saved them. Aware the village dogs were always hungry, she picked up the pouch and opened the drawstring. She thrust her hand inside, grabbed a handful of meat and threw it into the darkness towards the dogs. She continued this, scattering meat all about so that when the dogs caught its scent they savagely fell on it. They began to fight among themselves as larger dogs attempted to assert their superiority. When the pouch was empty Alna threw it away.

But then from the darkness came cries of alarm. The dogs had roused the village to the possibility of danger. The palisade had never been breached but there was always a first time. Such a fear was constantly in the villagers' minds, especially now with the threat from overseas raiders.

From his vantage point, Bolan could see the Assembly House. Men poured out down the steps from its wide entrance. Others followed carrying torches they had grabbed as they made their exit. For a moment they milled about and then Bolan saw Nevel. He was the tallest of all the village men. Now he took charge, gesticulating with his hands, the blazing torches throwing shadows on the Assembly House walls and on the ground. Men began to run in all directions, coming together again, armed now with spears, bows, arrows and even the digging sticks they used to break up the soil.

Bolan might never have taken his eyes from the sight if Vanu hadn't cried out again.

'Come on, Alna,' he whispered. 'We have to get away.' Bolan realised no one could hear him, such was the tumult made by the dogs and the villagers as they prepared to face whatever enemy might have got over the palisade.

'Tie the rope under Vanu's arms,' Bolan now shouted to Alna. 'Quickly! We've no time to lose.'

Bolan held the rope, ready to haul Vanu to the top of the palisade. When Alna had tied the rope she pushed Vanu to the foot of the buttress and urged him to climb.

Bolan was never more proud of his brother. Despite

his obvious fear, Vanu scrambled up the buttress, aided from above by Bolan. At the top of the palisade Bolan helped him over the spikes, hearing the child grunt with pain. But there was no time to lose. He quickly lowered Vanu to the ground outside the palisade, feeling the strain on his muscles and the burn on his palms as the rope slipped through his hands.

'Untie the rope, Vanu,' Bolan now ordered, but Vanu's little fingers could not undo the knots.

Already the clamour was growing louder as the group of armed men approached. They were being drawn to this very spot by the barking and yelping dogs frantically milling about in the darkness, seeking more meat.

Alna too was aware of the danger. She knew she had to climb the palisade next. Acting with great presence of mind, she threw the spear over the palisade, away from the spot where Vanu stood. The leister followed. Then she began to clamber up the buttress.

Dumb with fear, Bolan watched her, unable to help. She managed to climb a little way up the buttress before slipping back down again, desperately scrabbling with her arms and legs to gain a purchase. Again she tried but failed.

'Save yourself and Vanu,' she shouted at Bolan. 'Get away, before it's too late.'

Bolan felt his chest constrict. He could never have believed his sister could be so brave. She must have known that to remain meant certain death. But if he waited they would all die. Never before did he have to make such a decision. He only hesitated a moment. Bolan would never leave Alna. He would fight to the death.

He reached for his bow but just then Vanu called his name and he felt a tug on the rope, which he still held in his hand.

'Bolan,' Vanu called out again, his voice trembling with fear, 'you can pull up the rope now.'

Bolan did not need any encouragement. He pulled up the rope, noting that it still had a loop. Vanu had not been able to undo the knots so he had simply stepped out of the loop under his armpits. He was lucky, Bolan thought in that instant, to have such a brave, intelligent brother too.

Bolan dropped the rope down to Alna, who caught the loop in her hands, and she frantically began to climb towards Bolan. As she reached the top he helped her over the spikes and paid out the rope as she slid down to the ground on the other side.

At that moment the men, lead by Nevel, approached the palisade. There were about 40 of them, all armed. A few carried burning torches creating a grotesque tableau on the bare earth and on the logs of the palisade.

As soon as the men saw the milling dogs they relaxed. Most were still snuffling in the dust, searching for food and snapping at each other. Three of the bigger dogs were tearing the pouch asunder as if it were prey they held between their jaws.

This gave Bolan his opportunity. While the men were occupied watching the dogs, he hooked his bow on his shoulder. Then, grasping the rope in both hands, he clambered to the ground. His first instinct was to run. But he held his fear in check. The grappling hook was still caught on top of a spike and he wanted to know if Nevel saw it – or if he were suspicious of what was happening. With this in mind, Bolan crouched down, staring through a chink in the logs.

Nevel was clearly worried. He strode about, kicking out at the dogs who cringed away. Using his spear, he prodded at the dogs savaging the pouch. They reluctantly released it, growling threateningly. Nevel picked up the shredded pouch and examined it.

'A dog must have stolen a pouch of meat from one of the houses,' a man suggested.

Most of the others agreed with this. But Nevel did not speak. Bolan watched him as he strode about, the pouch in his hand. He stooped to examine the ground, but the earth was baked hard by the summer sun. He could read nothing there.

'It's just the dogs fighting over the meat,' another man suggested again. 'No one's got into the village. If they had done, the dogs would be tearing them apart right now. Let's go back to the Assembly House.'

A murmur of agreement greeted this. Nevel raised no objection and the men drifted away. Nevel, along with Bador, his closest ally, remained behind. Bolan knew Nevel was not happy.

Both men began to argue. Bador suggested they return to the Assembly House and resume their waking of Faver. Nevel, on the other hand, was still suspicious.

'I'm worried about Bolan,' he said. 'He knows we killed Faver and that his family is in danger. I don't trust him.'

'But he's only a child,' Bador said reassuringly.

'He's dangerous,' Nevel said. 'You know he's one of the finest hunters in the village. He's fearless and how can we know how a fearless man will act? Especially when he and his family are threatened.'

'But he's sick,' Bador protested.

'I don't think he is,' Nevel said. 'He was only pretending.'

'OK then,' Bador said, resigned. 'Let's check on him.

We'll kill them all now. Why wait until tomorrow?'
With that they moved off.

Outside the palisade Bolan held his breath and then let it out in a desperate sigh. He had made the right choice to leave but the danger was only beginning. In a few moments Nevel would know they had escaped. He would also know what had alarmed the dogs and what the significance of the pouch was. Within minutes they would be hunted.

There was no time to lose. If they did not escape into the forest right now, they would have failed before the perilous journey even rightly began.

3

LAYING A FALSE TRAIL

It was much darker in the forest than in the village, as the towering trees shut out the night sky. Underfoot, rotting leaves and vegetation made the ground as soft and springy as moss. Saplings grew in profusion – oak, beech and birch, thin stems pushing upwards, greedy for sunlight. Hawthorn and blackthorn grew here also along with alder, hazel and elder. In places, bracken grew to the height of a man, while brambles crawled in every direction, forming impenetrable barriers in places.

Bolan led the way, at times agonisingly slowly. Brambles snatched at them at every step and Bolan was relieved he had insisted on them all wearing leggings. The leggings were of beaver skin, wrapped tightly about the legs and tied with leather thongs. They offered some protection from the sharp thorns. Such precautions were necessary because a wound could easily become infected. Even a simple scratch, if left untreated, could lead to certain death.

Bolan was aware they were leaving a trail that would be easy to follow, even in the dark. Nevel and his men, if they dared venture out of the village tonight, would soon be in pursuit. When Bolan had decided to flee the village, he had been relying on making a head start. He also hoped that Nevel would not know from which direction they had left the village. But now Nevel knew the exact spot where they had scaled the palisade.

Bolan's original plan had been to head for the river. There he hoped to lose any pursuers by entering the water and leaving no trail to be followed.

At first Bolan panicked – he had been anxious to gain the shelter of the forest and wanted to get as far away as possible from the village. He had been worried too about the loss of their meat. But now he thrust that worry away. For the present he needed to concentrate on avoiding possible pursuers. Once they were safe from Nevel that was enough for now.

Fear of the forest and of the spirits which were said to roam there faded in the face of these new dilemmas. Bolan also feared animals who might see them as prey. But right now, all of his concentration was channelled into proceeding. At some stage, however, he would have to devise a plan. If he did not do so, Nevel would soon catch them.

Bolan led the children on, beating the brambles aside with his spear. Now and then he met an impenetrable barrier and was forced to make a detour. It was strenuous work and soon his muscles ached. But he did not dare rest. From time to time he stopped to listen for the sounds of pursuit. But there was none.

The forest was not silent. The trees creaked like the stiff joints of aging men and above them the leaves rustled in the wind. All around them smaller animals scurried hither and thither in the undergrowth. Screams of terror echoed through the dark occasionally as an animal fell prey to a predator.

Bolan reasoned it would take Nevel time to persuade the men to carry out his orders. They would be terrified of venturing into the forest after dark. They were also used to taking orders from Gaelan. This would be Nevel's first real attempt to exert his authority. If Nevel did not get the men to obey him now, he was doomed.

'We can't continue blundering on like this,' Bolan told Alna and Vanu. 'We're leaving a trail that will be easy to follow.'

'Could we hide somewhere?' Alna suggested.

'Not here,' Bolan said. 'Nevel would easily find our hideout. Even the darkness isn't on our side. Nevel knows the exact spot where we entered the forest. He'll have torches too and many men and they'll be able to travel much more quickly.'

'They'll catch us,' Vanu said. 'And then they'll kill us.' He was on the point of weeping.

Alna put her arm about his shoulders and comforted him. 'We'll be OK, Vanu,' she reassured the little boy. 'Bolan will get us away to safety.'

In the dark, Bolan shivered under the weight of responsibility thrust upon him. Today he had already had to make one difficult decision. Now he had another to make. Who could tell how many other decisions he might have to make before they reached Sarnay?

Bolan reconsidered his original plan of heading for the river. But in which direction did the river lie? They had made so many twists and turns that he had lost all sense of direction. The thought came to him that they could even be heading back towards the village, straight into the hands of Nevel.

Bolan was scared but to encourage the others he told them he had devised a plan – only his mind was devoid of ideas.

For once, luck was on their side. They had hardly

walked 200 paces when they came on a large clearing. Bolan did not know what had caused the clearing. Perhaps it had been created in an attempt by people like his own ancestors to settle here. No trace of them remained though. It reminded Bolan of what might become of his own village if his mission failed.

In all probability the clearing had been created by lightning. A tree was probably struck and set on fire, burning a huge area of forest, before rain put out the fires. Now, Bolan could again see the sky.

Before his grandfather's death, Bolan and the old man had been close. It was his grandfather who had told him about Sarnay and of the villages that lay along the course of the river. He had taught him about the spirits that controlled the earth and the sky and the forest. He had pointed out the stars to him so that Bolan knew the night sky as he knew his own village. Now he turned about until the stars he could see from the village when he looked towards the river were facing him. He knew the river lay in that direction. How far did they have yet to travel to reach it? Bolan could not even guess.

Luck was certainly on their side though, for the clearing was egg shaped. The river lay somewhere beyond the narrower end of the egg. This meant they could travel a good way without much hindrance.

Also they would not leave as obvious a trail for Nevel to follow. This would gain them valuable time.

With a lighter step, Bolan led the way forward. The ground was flat and, though there were saplings growing strongly here and brambles grew too in much more profusion, they were able to make good progress. When they reached the edge of the clearing Bolan stopped to listen. But there was still no sound of pursuers.

Taking a last bearing from the stars, Bolan plunged on into the forest again. And almost immediately he came upon the trail which went from Marn to the other villages along the river and on to Sarnay. This was the trail they needed to avoid. He could be certain Nevel would send some of his men along here to cut them off. But would he have done so already?

Bolan knew Nevel was a man of action, not of guile. His instinct would be to set off in pursuit. Right now there should be no danger ahead. The danger lay behind them.

A plan, hazy at first, but quickly becoming clearer, began to form in Bolan's mind. But for it to work he would have to leave Vanu behind. He and Alna would have to move quickly and Vanu's presence would only hinder them.

'Are you tired?' Bolan now asked his brother.

'No,' Vanu said in a brave voice. 'I can still walk.'

Bolan swallowed. Not yet eight, Vanu was already

showing the bravery of his father.

'I'll tell you what,' Bolan said. 'I'll give you a ride on my back, as a reward for being so brave.'

With that, Bolan crouched down and Vanu climbed on his back, clasping his hands about his brother's neck. Then they moved forward again, keeping to the trail which was only wide enough for two to walk abreast. They remained silent, preserving their breath for more important tasks. Bolan was seeking a tree for his plan. But none seemed suitable. With each step his already tired muscles ached all the more and Vanu seemed to become heavier. Bolan knew he could not carry his brother much further.

But just when his strength was about to give out he came on the very tree he sought. It was a giant oak, centuries old, its branches crossing right over the track a little above the height of a man. Bolan stopped.

'See this tree?' he asked Vanu. 'Would you like to climb it?'

'Oh yes,' Vanu said, unable to resist.

'Stand on my shoulders then,' Bolan suggested. 'Grab the branch and climb onto it. From there you must climb high up into the tree. Alna and I will go on. But we'll come back for you. I will hoot like an owl so you will know that it is us. Now you mustn't make a sound and you must be very brave.'

Alna didn't question Bolan's motives. She knew this was not some game he was playing. She helped steady Vanu as he stood on Bolan's shoulders and reached for the overhanging branch. For one perilous moment Vanu almost toppled to the ground. But somehow, with Alna's help, Bolan managed to hold his brother upright, straining under the weight on his shoulders. As Vanu grabbed the branch and pulled himself upwards, scrabbling for a foothold, he stood on Bolan's head, causing him to gasp with pain. But a moment later Vanu was safely on the branch and, at Bolan's urging, was clambering higher into the tree.

'There's no time to lose,' Bolan told Alna. 'We must lay a false trail.'

They hurried forward, keeping to the trail for a few hundred paces. Then Bolan plunged back into the forest, heading for the river. Alna was aware they were again leaving an easy trail for Nevel to follow. But she did not speak.

Soon they emerged from the forest only to be confronted by what appeared to be a giant black writhing snake. It was the river, which was wide and shallow here, the low water level a result of the fine summer.

'We'll go into the water,' Bolan told Alna. 'That way we'll leave no trail for Nevel to follow.'

Alna nodded and Bolan led the way into the river.

It was icy cold and they both gasped as the water level came halfway up their calves. They waded out a little way to avoid the overhanging branches of the poplars and birches which grew along the bank.

Here Bolan turned upstream much to Alna's surprise. The current was not strong here but nevertheless it was not easy to wade against it.

'Shouldn't we be going downstream,' Alna whispered but Bolan shook his head and kept going up river against the flow of the water.

Soon Alna began to shiver and her teeth chattered. But she clenched them tightly, thinking of how brave Vanu had been to remain behind all alone. She forced herself to keep going forward, stifling a scream of sheer terror when something struck her leg. It was probably a piece of driftwood but she was convinced it was a giant pike and that it would sink its teeth into her flesh. It took all her courage to stay calm and not strike out for the safety of the riverbank.

The river swung to the left in a sweeping bend and here the water ran more slowly. They waded on until they negotiated the bend and the river again ran straight as an arrow.

'By now we should be well past the tree where Vanu is hiding,' Bolan said to Alna. 'So we'll leave the river and make our way back to the trail.'

'Ah, now I see what you've been doing,' Alna said, her voice filled with admiration for Bolan. 'Nevel will follow our trail to the river. He'll think that you carried Vanu all the way and that we've now gone downstream. He'll search both banks for evidence of where we left the river. But of course he'll find none. Then he won't know where we are.'

'He'll figure it our eventually,' Bolan said. 'But we'll have gained valuable time. Now we must get back to Vanu without delay.'

They emerged from the river, their wet leggings clinging to their skin, and headed back into the forest. Soon they came upon the trail. The bend in the river had brought them close to it. They huddled at the edge of the trail, concealed by the undergrowth, listening for any sound of Nevel or his men. But there seemed to be none.

Bolan stood up and was about to move onto the trail when a man called out and was answered by another. Bolan froze, turning his head to try and catch the direction from which the calls had come. Again a man called out. The sound came from the direction of the village. Bolan had miscalculated Nevel's intelligence. He must have sent some of his men to try and head them off while others took up direct pursuit.

Bolan hesitated, thinking quickly. What if some men had already gone ahead? But that was a risk they would have to face. Now it was imperative that they reach the tree where Vanu was hidden.

Making as little noise as possible, Bolan crept from the undergrowth. He was prepared for a warning shout but none came. He beckoned Alna and when she joined him they hurried forward. All about them the darkness seemed much thicker and more oppressive. But they hurried on, aching muscles forgotten as fear gave a freshness to their limbs.

When they reached the tree Bolan gave one owl hoot. Then Alna climbed on his shoulders and grasped the over-hanging branch. She pulled herself up and crawled along the branch to where it joined the trunk. From here she reached her hand down to Bolan. He grasped it and scrambled up the trunk, gaining handholds and footholds on bits of broken branches and new growth. Eventually he made it onto the branch but there was no time to lose. Already they could hear the sound of the pursuers as they drew near.

Bolan and Alna climbed higher into the tree until they joined Vanu. He was aware of the danger and remained silent. Below them the sound of the pursuers could now be heard clearly. Alna clutched Vanu to her and they held their breath as danger drew nearer and nearer.

4

THE HIDING PLACE

Bador led three men in the pursuing party. As they followed the trail they argued amongst themselves. They had no torches and Bolan saw them only as shapes in the darkness. He recognised Bador's voice. Bador was angry now and threatened his companions with violence if they did not remain with him. They wanted to return to the village and Bolan recognised fear in their voices.

Bolan was tempted to swing down from the tree and catch them unawares. In their fear and confusion, Bador's companions would be more of a hindrance than a help. But could he kill all three of them? If even one of them got away they would inform Nevel of the hiding place. Then Bolan, Alna and Vanu would have to flee again.

Bador and his companions were directly beneath the tree now and the three children crouched amongst the branches, holding their breaths. But Bador did not falter in his step. He went right past, followed by his grumbling companions. Eventually the voices faded and the noises of the forest took over again.

'That's one piece of luck,' Bolan whispered. 'They'll trample our footprints. It will help to confuse Nevel.'

'Does that mean we're safe now?' Vanu asked.

'You've nothing to fear,' Bolan said confidently, not wanting to alarm his brother. But he was aware that the dangers, far from being over, had not yet really begun. He knew the traders who came from Sarnay took many days to make the journey.

'What do we do now?' Alna asked.

'We wait,' Bolan said. 'We're safe here.'

'But what about food?' Alna asked. 'The pouch we lost contained all our meat.'

'Don't worry about that,' Bolan said reassuringly. 'I'll get us more meat. Now we must rest. You and Vanu get some sleep. I'll keep watch.'

The oak tree had been growing for centuries and its branches would take the arms of two men to encircle them. Alna settled herself in a fork created by two branches and leaned back again the trunk. Then she had Vanu stretch out along the branch and lay his head in her lap. Within minutes he was asleep. Soon afterwards Alna too nodded off.

Bolan remained alert, his mind occupied with how they might safely get away to continue the journey to Sarnay. By now his father and the two men who had accompanied him would be close to the settlement. It would take them two or three days to conduct their business before they set out on the return journey. Nevel would strike then, probably taking them unawares one night while they slept. At best Bolan had about four days in which to make the journey. At worst he might have no more than three.

At this very moment they should be travelling. But it was impossible. The children could not venture out from their hideout. Bador was already ahead of them while Nevel must be fast gaining ground behind. If they went out they would be trapped between the two parties.

They could not remain here much longer though. They had little food and time was not on their side. At first light they would have to make a decision as to what to do next.

Bolan intended keeping watch all night but fatigue crept up on him and some time before dawn he nodded off. Voices woke him and at first he did not know where he was. For a moment he thought he was still back in the village. But reality quickly returned and he shook Alna and Vanu to waken them. He could not afford for them to wake suddenly and cry out or speak.

As they awoke, yawning and stretching to ease their cramped muscles, he motioned them to silence. But there was no need. Both Alna and Vanu could hear the voices of approaching men and knew it spelled danger.

The sound came from the direction of the village. Nevel and his men were approaching. Through the dense foliage the children watched them. There were three others with Nevel. All four were armed and alert. They drew near the tree and stopped to examine the ground.

'They came this way,' Nary said. He was the best tracker in Marn, an art that was dying out as the settlement more and more came to depend on its own resources. Bolan had not counted on Nary siding with Nevel. But there was nothing he could do about it now.

'Are they still carrying the boy?' Nevel asked.

'Yes,' Nary said. 'But the tracks aren't easy to read. Bador and his men have passed along here too. They've trampled the original footprints.'

'Fools,' Nevel shouted. 'I'm plagued by fools.' He struck one of the other men, who cringed away from him.

'They can't have got far,' Nary suggested. 'Even Bolan can't carry the boy forever. Perhaps Bador has already caught up with them and killed them.'

'I've forbidden him to kill Bolan,' Nevel said. 'I want that pleasure for myself. I want to teach the village a lesson. Once I've dealt with him no one will dare oppose me again.'

Bolan suppressed a shiver. Alna and Vanu stared at him with frightened eyes. But he forced himself to smile to reassure them.

'What do we do now?' Nary asked.

'We keep following them,' Nevel explained. 'We've plenty of time. We won't kill Gaelan until he's on his return from Sarnay. That gives us five days at least. If we can't capture three children in that time then we don't deserve to succeed. Now let's go on.' He struck out at the other two men who ran forward to avoid his fists. All four passed beneath the tree and went in the direction of Sarnay.

'What do we do now?' Alna asked. 'We can't go on. They'll be waiting up ahead for us.' Her voice was fearful and Vanu drew closer to her.

'Right now we eat,' Bolan said lightly. 'We can't do anything on an empty stomach.'

But fear had taken away their appetites and they merely nibbled some oatcakes. They were dry and hard and they washed them down with water from the pigskin pouch. All about them the morning became lighter as the sun rose higher in the sky. It was going to be another scorching day. But in the tree they were sheltered from the direct sunlight and it was cool.

The forest was alive with sound. Birds sang and squabbled, taking over from the night chorus. Animals still scurried about in the undergrowth. Now and then butterflies flitted through shafts of sunshine which penetrated the canopy of foliage here and there.

The sun climbed higher still, slowly marking out the passage of time. Vanu fell asleep and soon Alna too succumbed to fatigue. Bolan was on the point of drifting off when he again heard men approaching. It was Nevel and the men returning. They stopped close to the tree and it was clear from his voice that Nevel was angered by their failure.

'We'll return to the village,' he ordered, 'and get provisions. If you had done your job there would be no need for this. How could you let three children make a fool of you?'

'It's not my fault,' Bador complained. 'They reached the river before us and we couldn't pick up their trail again. But they can't have got far. They missed the coracle which the villagers of Insk keep there for crossing the river. Or else they were too frightened to take it. So they're still on foot. Vanu is tired or hurt and they have little food. They're in hiding somewhere along the riverbank but we'll find them when they venture out. They can't remain hidden forever.'

'Go back then and search for them,' Nevel ordered. 'Take Nary with you. We'll join you later.'

'But we've no food or water,' Bador wailed. 'Can't we return to the village with you? It's dangerous for two men to be alone in the forest.'

Nevel laughed maliciously. 'Surely you're not scared,' he said, and the others sniggered at Bador's discomfort.

'I'm not frightened,' Bador said angrily and he struck at a clump of bracken with his spear.

'Then go back to the river,' Nevel commanded. 'Find their trail again. And remember, Bolan is mine. He's not to be harmed.'

With that they split up. Bador and Nary turned back. Nevel and the others passed directly beneath the oak tree, heading for the village. As they passed, Nevel glanced upwards. His eyes and those of Bolan seemed to meet. Bolan reached for his bow which lay beside him. But then he realised that Nevel could not see him. His fear was making him imagine things.

Bolan gave the villagers sufficient time to get away

from the area. Only then did he suggest they leave their hiding place. A new idea was forming in his mind. If it worked then they would get away safely.

He knew his idea was fraught with danger. None of them could swim. But if they remained here Nevel would capture them. He would eventually figure out how they had fooled him. Then he would turn out all the village men to search for them. Their only hope lay in getting away. There were only two men up ahead. If they waited much longer there might be ten or twelve to face.

Bolan climbed down first to check for danger. When he was satisfied there was none, Alna and Vanu joined him. They set off again, moving quickly but stealthily. At the point where he'd turned off the trail last night, Bolan struck out for the river. He knew it was their only hope now of getting safely away.

5

A VIOLENT ENCOUNTER

They reached the river without mishap. As they approached the bank Alna and Vanu hid in the under-growth while Bolan went forward alone, taking only his spear. He kept a sharp look out for Bador and Nary. But there was no sign of them. They had almost certainly gone on further down stream.

What Bolan sought for the planned getaway was the coracle Bador had found somewhere about here. But Bolan had to find it quickly. It was obviously close by because the trail that led to Insk was visible on the farther bank. About 100 paces downstream were the remains of the bridge which had once stood here.

Alert for danger, Bolan began to make his way along the riverbank. He was following the tracks made by Bador, his eyes seeking the coracle which must be hidden somewhere along here. He passed the spot opposite the trail to Insk and continued on for another 200 paces. But he found no sign of a boat.

It was then Bolan realised that Bador and Nary may have taken the boat and were already on the river. He had gambled on the boat being here. Right now Nevel was certainly on his way back, his heart blackened with murderous rage and his mind set on vengeance.

Bolan was on the verge of panic, with no idea of how to proceed. He had led them all into a trap. They could neither go forward nor back. Once Nevel caught the scent, he would beat the forest until there was no place to hide. Bolan had been on the hunt often enough to know how an animal was cornered and killed.

He stared across the river, his mind working like that of a cornered animal. Would they be safer on the farther bank? Or was the wide stretch of water no more than an illusory protection? The trail to Insk beckoned him. But to go that way would achieve nothing. Even if they reached Insk, Nevel would come for them. The people of Insk would not wish to quarrel with Marn and would hand them over.

Anxiously, Bolan turned to make his way back to Alna and Vanu. Their only hope now lay in returning to the oak tree and hiding until nightfall. Perhaps with darkness on their side they could slip past what-ever guards Nevel would place on the trail.

At the spot opposite the Insk trail Bolan stopped again and stared across the river. And it was then he saw the boat. It was tied up on the far bank, partly hidden by a fallen tree. He let out a long sigh of relief and silently reproached himself for not having realised the boat could be on the other side. His apprehension was clouding his judgement and he would have to ensure it did not happen again.

Buoyed up with hope, Bolan waded into the river. Despite the sunshine, the water was still icy cold. His damp leggings were immediately saturated and clung to his calves. But he waded on. As he reached the cen-tre of the river the depth of the water increased. Here too the current was quite strong and he was finding it difficult to keep his balance.

Bolan stopped by one of the remaining oak piles which had supported the bridge. He found a hand-hold on a smaller piece of timber attached to the pile and held on. The bank still seemed as far away as ever, and the boat remained unattainable. He stared into the water, trying to see the bottom. But with the glare of the sun off the water it was impossible. He could not know if the river would get deeper. Yet there was only one way to find out. He would have to go forward.

He pushed forwards against the water, gingerly feeling for the bottom. A few steps took him away from the pile and he had to release his hold. He waded on and the water level still rose. It reached his waist and he began to experience panic. He imagined himself toppling over and the water swamping him, filling his lungs so he could not breathe, stifling his cries for help. He gripped his spear more tightly and forced himself to take another step. Then he took another and another but the water level did not rise again. He had reached the deepest part of the river.

With this realisation came a burst of courage and he waded on. As the water level dropped to knee height he found a burst of energy and made the far bank at a run, for one joyous moment not caring about the noise he was making.

There was no time to waste and he checked the boat straightaway. It was a small coracle which would carry four men. The frame was woven from willow, covered with leather and caulked with pitch. But there were no oars. Bolan realised the villagers would have taken the oars with them so the boat could not be used.

He needed something to use as an oar. Once they were on the river, the current would carry them along. But first he had to cross to the other side to pick up Alna and Vanu. There was no way they would be able to wade across as he had.

Bolan wished he had brought his axe with him. But all he had was the spear. He glanced at it, wondering if he could fashion a makeshift oar from it. He searched around for a suitable piece of timber and eventually found a branch of a tree, as thick as his arm and half as long. Taking careful aim, he drove the spear into the branch halfway along its length. He checked that it was held firmly, then untied the coracle and climbed aboard.

Using the makeshift oar, he pushed the coracle out from beneath the tree. Once he was clear of the obstacle he found it was more difficult to manoeuvre the boat than he had thought at first. As he paddled, the boat simply made circles in the water. But once he realised he should paddle from either side alternately he made progress.

As Bolan reached the centre of the river the current increased. He had to paddle furiously but even then the river began to carry him downstream. He kept his eye on the spot where he had first entered the water and it seemed as though it was drifting upstream while he remained stationary.

But Bolan did not panic. He kept furiously paddling

and so slowly began to beat the current. He passed the point where the current was strongest and was soon making headway upstream. His arms were aching by the time he reached the far bank but he could not delay. He leapt from the boat and tied it to the overhanging branch of a poplar. Then he went to find Alna and Vanu.

Hurriedly the three children piled into the boat, stowing their provisions and gear. Once they were settled, Bolan paddled out to the centre of the river. He was becoming more adept with the oar and they were soon in the current, being borne downstream. Bolan had little to do with the oar now except keep the boat in a straight line.

For the first time since they left the village they could relax. Alna and Vanu chattered about what they saw – the water vole that swam parallel to them for a while, its head raised proudly above the water. Swarms of flies hung above the river like falling rain when seen against the glare of the sun. Swallows fed on the largesse, swooping in low, skimming the surface to bank away again for yet another flight. Trout rose to feed, their bodies arched in the air like bent bows. On either side the forest slowly drifted backwards. At one point Bolan had to negotiate a tree which must have been swept downstream when the river was in torrent. But otherwise there was nothing to hinder their progress.

Bolan untied his wet leggings and hung them over the side to dry. He was enjoying the warmth of the sun on his face, certain they were out of danger for the present. They must have left Bador and Nary far behind them now.

So when they heard the warning shout, it startled him all the more. It came from up ahead and Bolan, who was hunched forward, beginning to feel the effects of fatigue, shot bolt upright. The sun was high in the sky but the glare off the water seemed to shine directly in his eyes. He shielded them with his hand and only then saw Bador. He was on the right-hand bank almost directly opposite. Bolan's blood seemed to freeze in his veins despite the warmth. He grabbed his bow and felt for an arrow. Bador caught the movement and, aware of Bolan's reputation as a bowman, drew back into the undergrowth. Bolan never took his eyes from the spot, watching for any movement that would betray Bador or his intentions. Alna too watched the spot, her whole being filled with dread. And so it was that it was left to Vanu to save them.

They had forgotten all about Nary. But unknown to them, Nary had been searching for their trail on the farther bank and had been roused by Bador's warning shout. Nary had spotted the coracle and recognised the occupants. Gripping his spear in his hands he had waded into the stream to intercept the frail craft.

It was Vanu who saw Nary. At first the little boy was too frightened to cry out. But as they headed straight towards Nary, Vanu shouted a warning.

It was almost too late. Even as Bolan followed Vanu's pointing finger, Nary threw his spear. It was aimed at Bolan's head and would have entered his skull, embedding itself in his brain and killing him instantly if he had been a split second too slow. But as Bolan violently ducked sideways he heard the swish of the spear as it flew harmlessly through the air and fell with a splash in the river.

Nary froze when he realised he had missed his target. Then, as he saw Bolan recover, he roused himself and desperately made for the illusory safety of the bank. But he was too late. Bolan raised the bow and sighted his eye along the arrow. He allowed for the movement of the boat and then released the arrow.

They heard the twang of the bow and the whiz of the arrow through the shimmering air. In the same instant they heard a squelch and Nary's cry as the flint arrow-head buried itself in his thigh. Bolan had not intended killing Nary. He only wanted to incapacitate him.

Nary's hands grabbed the hazel shaft and he swayed as if blown by a wind. He lurched, moaning, to the riverbank where he toppled over, writhing in pain. The three children watched him as the boat slid past, bearing them to safety. Further back they could hear the helpless angry cries of Bador.

Bolan turned to look and saw Bador, who had emerged from his hiding place. Bolan reached for another arrow and just then, somewhere ahead, a blackbird burst into song. Bolan drew his hand away empty. There had been enough violence.

He faced forward again as the boat beat on down-river towards Sarnay. On they drifted with the current, away from danger – away from the awful reminder of violence. But Bolan was aware that more danger and maybe more violence lay waiting for them.

6

A STORM BREAKS

The incident had shaken them. Alna held Vanu close to her, comforting him and taking comfort for herself. Bolan stared down the length of the river, his ears still filled with the squelching sound of the arrow striking home. After a while he roused himself and began again to keep a lookout for obstacles. If they struck one it could tear the boat open and sink it. If they ended up in the water they were doomed.

For a long time they did not speak. But slowly the sunshine drove the chill of fear from them and they began to discuss what they should do.

'We must stay on the river,' Bolan said. 'When Nevel hears of our getaway and the injury to Nary he'll be furious and will pursue us. Only he won't be able to travel as quickly as we can on the river. Our best chance of success now is to stay ahead of him.'

'But we won't be able to travel at night,' Alna said, with concern. 'It would be too dangerous. And we'll need to rest.'

'I know that,' Bolan said.

'And what about food?' she asked.

'I'm hungry,' Vanu piped up. 'And I'm thirsty too.'

'We'll eat now then,' Bolan said. 'So let's forget about Nevel for the moment.' But as the food was handed out, he could not banish Nevel from his mind. Nor prevent himself from glancing backwards, as if danger lurked just behind them.

They had oatcakes again and bread spread with wild honey, all washed down with water. Afterwards they ate fruit, mostly wild strawberries and raspberries. With their hunger satisfied, they began to grow languid in the sunshine. It was becoming warmer as the day progressed. Whatever breeze there had been was stilled and the air was growing heavy and humid. There appeared to be less activity too. The forest was still and the birds seemed too lazy to fly. Only the river became more active, with fish rising all about the boat to feast on the swarms of flies.

Bolan grew uneasy and every few moments glanced skywards. The sky was becoming blotched with ragged cloud. At the horizon a darker line of cloud could be seen. As they drifted on a herd of deer came downriver to the riverbank to drink. They looked uneasy, and milled about the bank as if the scent of a predator was on the air.

But Bolan knew it was not a predator they feared. He had been taught to read the signs of nature – the colour and shape of clouds, the direction of the wind, the behaviour of animals. From the signs he saw all about him he knew a storm was brewing. The anger of the great Spirit of the Sky was about to be unleashed.

Bolan's people believed that the sky and earth were ruled by two great spirits. At Marn they had a shrine to the Earth Spirit who made the soil fertile. Here, their priest made sacrifices to ensure a rich harvest. If the harvest should fail, famine and death were inevitable.

It was the duty of every person at Marn to keep the spirits appeased. If the spirits were at ease, harmony existed. But sometimes the spirits were angered, and when this occurred, their fury knew no bounds.

Bolan knew the spirits had been angered when Nevel killed Faver. Now their rage was about to be unleashed. Soon the Spirit of the Sky would strike at the forest with bolts of fire and the sound of his blows would rumble across the heavens.

Meanwhile, the Earth Spirit would fill the rivers to

overflowing. They would in turn burst their banks and flood the village. Fields too would be flooded and crops destroyed. Sometimes animals and even people would be swept away to their deaths.

Bolan knew the anger of the spirits would hinder their progress. But it would hinder Nevel too. He would not dare to travel while the spirits raged. Even he would be frightened of their wrath. He would have to shelter until the storm blew over.

Now, as the coracle drifted on, clouds continued to build up. Eventually they blotted out the sun, bringing a premature twilight. Bolan decided to press on. He would wait until the storm broke before coming off the river.

But their progress was not halted by the storm. It was halted instead by a village, similar to Marn but much larger. As they slipped round a bend in the river they saw the palisade, some thousand paces ahead. The village was built on both sides of the river and the palisade encircled it, cutting across the river itself. Gaps had been left between the logs so as not to impede the flow of the water. But the gaps were too narrow for a person to pass through.

All Bolan's attention had been focused on the weather. But now it was alerted to this new danger. If the villagers spotted them, they might be attacked.

Bolan gripped his makeshift oar more tightly and began to paddle furiously to try and force the coracle out of the current towards the left-hand bank

But the current was quite strong and the boat continued to drift on towards the village. Closer now, Bolan could see the village fields outside the palisade. Men were herding cattle towards the palisade, bringing them into a safe haven before the storm struck. He was certain the men would see them, but they were too occupied with their task to notice.

Alna became aware of their predicament. She leaned over the side of the boat and used her hand as a paddle. Vanu too helped. Slowly they edged the coracle out of the current. Once it was free of the pull of the river, they quickly reached the safety of the bank. They drifted in under the overhanging alder branches, ducking their heads low. The water was shallow and Bolan leapt from the boat and helped the other two on to the bank. All three now helped to pull the boat up out of the water, dragging it back from the edge so it was concealed from the village.

'We'll have to wait until it's dark,' Bolan told the others, 'before we can slip by the village. So before the storm breaks, I'll try and catch us some fish.'

Alna and Vanu nodded. Bolan took his leister and moved off up the river. A little further back he'd noticed a spot where the bank had been eroded away, toppling trees into the water. It had formed a small pool which seemed an ideal spot for river trout.

When he got there he waded into the water until it reached his calves. He stood quite still, allowing the disturbance he had made to settle. Without the glare of the sun off the water he could see the sandy bottom of the river once his eyes adjusted to the seemingly impenetrable murk.

The river teemed with fish and he saw them dart hither and thither. But they were small. He wanted one or two large trout. A fine pike would be more acceptable but he did not think this was a good spot for one of those fearsome fish.

So when he saw the pike he was struck motionless for a moment. It nosed into his range of vision, as long as his arm, its pointed head with those teeth sharp as flint moving languidly from side to side as it sought a prey. For a moment it lay still and Bolan gripped the haft of the leister more tightly. Then, with a powerful flick of its tail, the pike struck. As it caught its prey, it broke the surface. Bolan had a momentary view of its white underbelly and then he was striking at that vulnerable spot with the prongs of the leister.

Long hours of patience and practice paid off as the

pike was speared. It made desperate efforts to escape but the prongs of the leister held it firm. Slowly its struggle eased but Bolan was not fooled. From experience he knew the fish would make a last desperate effort to escape. He had known one villager who had thought a pike was dead and who had had his hand ripped open when he tried to take his catch from the water.

The pike struggled but already its strength was fading. Bolan knew he had it. Carefully he edged it to the bank and brought it onto dry land. The pike lay on its side with its mouth open, displaying its fearsome teeth, the trout it had caught still wedged in its jaws. It thrashed feebly and with the haft of the leister Bolan killed it. Then he picked it up and bore it back to where Alna and Vanu waited.

They were both overjoyed to see the fish which Bolan expertly gutted and cleaned with his flint dagger. He also gutted the trout and that too would be eaten. As he worked it grew darker still. Soon the storm would be upon them.

'We'll move back into the forest,' Bolan suggested. 'I'll light a fire and cook the fish. No one will notice the smoke in this murk.'

They moved back into the shelter of the trees where they found a small clearing. Using the fire-starting flints and tinder, Bolan soon had a tiny flickering flame licking the dried grass and small twigs he piled around and on top of it. By taking care not to smother the flames, the fire gave off little more than a few wisps of smoke.

Alna and Vanu gathered sticks and soon the fire was blazing. When it had a glowing heart, Bolan placed the pike and the trout on the embers. Immediately the oil from the fish began to sizzle and a mouth-watering smell wafted into their nostrils. They looked at each other and grinned, all danger and hardship forgotten for a moment.

When the fish were cooked Bolan removed them from the fire which was now dying out. He expertly removed the vertebrae and cut the fish into portions. All three ate their fill and then licked their fingers clean. Alna took what remained and placed it in the pouch which contained the bread and oatcakes.

Just then rain began to fall, sizzling on the dying embers like the drops of oil had.

'Come,' Bolan commanded. 'We must shelter.'

'We could use the boat,' Alna suggested. 'If we turn it upside down we can shelter beneath it.'

'Great idea,' Bolan said, and he led the way back to the river. They manoeuvred the coracle across to where two alders grew close together. They wedged the boat between the tree trunks, the stern resting on the ground, the prow pointing at an angle towards the sky.

They gathered their belongings and piled them at the stern. Then they got in under the upturned craft. They were only just in time. The rain came in a great torrent, beating like pebbles on the boat's taut skin. But they were well sheltered and hardly a drop struck them.

The storm rolled towards them. Lightning ripped across the sky. The thunder became an almost continuous rumble, growing louder and louder until it was directly above their heads. The rain intensified and the murk became thicker. All about the air was heavy and cloying.

Across the river a tree was struck by lightning. They heard the crack when the trunk was split open as if by a blow from a giant axe. There was an acrid smell on the air as the wood burnt and the sap boiled like water in the intense heat.

It was a stark reminder of the dangers of being in the forest when the spirits were angry. Alna clutched Vanu to her and felt his body tremble in time with her own.

'Tell us a story, Bolan,' she said. 'I'm sure Vanu would love to hear one.'

Bolan stared at them and sensed their fear. It was a mirror image of his own. He pushed his fear aside and smiled.

'What story shall I tell you?' he asked.

'Tell us about our mother,' Alna said. 'Vanu loves to hear you talk about her.'

Bolan nodded, closing his eyes and drifting back in his mind to a time when he had known no fear.

'Her name was Alanna,' he began. 'She was tall and slender, unlike the other village women. Her hair was long and dark, just like Vanu's, and she was very proud of it. She combed it every day and kept it in place with a wooden clasp. At festival time she would plait it and wear a garland of flowers.

'All the village children loved her. They would come to our house and she'd give them oatcakes spread with honey. We'd all play together and she would join us. She'd hide and we'd have to find her. Sometimes she would sing and her voice was sweeter than any birds. I never knew where she learned the songs but later my father told me she made them up herself.

'She taught me one of her songs. Even still I remember it.' Bolan paused and began to sing. The song had both words and sounds, a sort of plaintive chant that rose and fell as the lightning flashed and the thunder rumbled across the sky.

As the song finished he saw himself in his mind's eye as a child again, running to his mother. She clasped him to her and he smelled the honeysuckle blossom she had entwined in her hair. Her shining dark eyes were laughing as she handed him over to his father.

His father's arms were strong and firm. Bolan felt the power of them as he was hoisted in the air and caught as he fell, his cry of pleasure and fear ringing in his ears. Again and again he was hoisted and caught until his fear was no more.

Bolan was wrapped in his memories when a hand touched his arm. He shook himself and returned to the present.

'Vanu's asleep,' Alna said. 'Telling him about our mother has rid him of his fear.'

'Good,' Bolan said. 'Now you too must sleep.'

While Alna slept, the storm slowly passed. Lightning no longer rent the sky and the thunder faded to a distant rumble. But the rain continued to beat down relentlessly and the air remained still and heavy. And all this time Bolan crouched beneath the boat, waiting for the spirit's anger to burn itself out and the world to return to normal.

7

TRAPPED BY WATER

Fatigue eventually overcame Bolan and he too slept. When he awoke he stretched his cramped muscles and ducked out from beneath the boat, not wishing to wake the others. The rain had ceased and no longer hammered down on the boat. But another sound had replaced it. From twenty paces away came the roar of the river in full flood.

Dawn was just beginning to lighten the sky. The sun had not yet risen but the sky was suffused with a pinkish glow. Soon it would be daylight and an urgency gripped Bolan. It was imperative that they get past the village before then.

Bolan walked down to the flood-swollen river. Where they had left the boat yesterday was now under water. Further out on the river all kinds of debris was being borne along on the seething torrent and at the sight of it, his heart sank. Even if they could drag the boat past the village, it would be the height of folly to venture on the river. The frail craft would not survive the flood water never mind the debris which would rip it open.

They would have to travel on foot again. That meant they must leave immediately. Bolan returned to the makeshift shelter, the ground soggy underfoot. Any place that was muddy easily took footprints. It was something else they would have to consider. They would leave a clear trail for Nevel to follow.

Bolan woke Alna and Vanu. They were stiff and uncomfortable from the cramped positions in which they had slept.

'I'm sorry,' Bolan said, saddened at the sight of Vanu yawning, his little face pinched with discomfort. 'But we must get past the village before daylight. So we have to leave immediately.'

'Will we be going on the river again?' Vanu asked. The prospect of travelling in the boat excited him and made him forget his discomfort.

'Not now,' Bolan said. 'But maybe later.'

'Is that the river I hear?' Alna asked.

Bolan nodded. They exchanged glances and Alna knew

they could not travel on the river again. They would have to try and outrun Nevel on foot. The thought struck fear into her but she did her best to hide it.

'We must eat now,' Bolan said. 'Then we'll leave.'

They had a meagre breakfast, eating a little of the fish along with some bread. Already more than half of their bread ration was gone. Bolan was aware of this but did not mention it. The other two had enough worries without him adding to them.

When they had eaten Bolan led them down to the riverbank. Here they washed their faces and hands with water that was murky from the mud washed down by the floods. They then gathered their possessions together and set off, keeping clear of the river bank, using the trees and scrub as cover. The sky was brightening all the time and soon the sun would rise above the treetops.

The village was on their right and they skirted the palisade, at times having to hack their way through the undergrowth. All about them birds were beginning to sing but in their urgency the children hardly noticed this. On they plunged, glimpsing the palisade from time to time.

Eventually through a break in the trees they saw they had reached the end of the palisade. Here the river emerged from the village, the wild headlong rush of the water impeded somewhat by the obstacle in its path.

Bolan stopped to look. All seemed quiet. They still had time on their side. With luck they could still evade Nevel. But they must press on. Bolan led them off again, deciding that once they were well past the village, he would lead them away from the river. By now Nevel would know they had taken the coracle. He would realise when he arrived at the village here that they would not have been able to travel any further on the river. So he would search for the coracle at the point where the river entered the village. Working back upstream meant he would locate the boat and learn where they had camped overnight. He would know then that they could not be too far away and, encouraged by this, he would take up the hunt with fresh vigour.

Bolan looked around nervously, careful not to let Alna or Vanu see that he was worried. But there was neither sight nor sound of pursuit. How long would that last though? He quickened his pace, twisting this way and that to find the easiest route. At one point they came upon the remains of a wild boar. As they approached, small creatures which had been feeding on the scraps of meat remaining on the bones scurried into the undergrowth. Some magpies sat on a nearby tree, awaiting their turn to scavenge the boar's carcass.

The animal had probably only been killed yester-day, almost certainly the victim of wolves. Bolan knew they roamed the forest in packs and would attack if driven by hunger. Only the bear was safe from their savagery.

They skirted the carcass and, once past, heard the rustling noise again as the smaller predators returned to their meal. The sight of the bones had shaken Bolan – it was as if they were an omen of what could happen to them all. If Nevel killed them he would take their heads back to the village as trophies and as a threat to others who might question his authority. But he would leave their bodies to the wolves and the smaller predators who would pick the bones clean.

What they needed now was another lucky break. But their luck was about to desert them. Quite sudden-ly they emerged from the forest to find the river block-ing their progress. They halted in dismay and stared in disbelief at the raging flood waters blocking their path.

'The river must change course here,' Alna said.

But Bolan shook his head.

'Look at the direction of the current,' he said. 'This is a different river. It must be a tributary of the Ohan.'

'Does that mean we have to cross it?' Alna asked, her voice trembling.

'We can't go forward unless we cross it,' Bolan

said. 'But we can't risk crossing it. It's much too dangerous. We'd be swept away.'

'So what will we do?' It was Vanu who asked. He was trying to hide his fear but it showed in his dark eyes.

'We must go back,' Bolan said. 'It's our only chance.'

'But Nevel ...' Alna caught his arm, her eyes pleading.

'He may not have reached the village yet,' Bolan said. 'So we've still got time. We must go back and hide in the forest. When the waters go down we can use the coracle to cross the river. It's our only chance.'

'But Nevel will surely find us,' Alna said, clearly scared.

'No!' Bolan swung about and gripped her arm in turn. Alna shrunk from him. She had never before seen him so determined. 'Nevel won't find us. He can't find us!' He spoke vehemently, his face implacably set. There could be no arguing with him.

In any event, there was little else they could do. If they did not get out of here quickly they would be trapped. Nevel and his men would simply close in on them, aware there was no place left to run.

8

A NARROW ESCAPE

As they retraced their footsteps towards danger and possible death, Bolan realised Nevel may learn about the second river from the villagers. He would realise then that the children were trapped and would close in quickly for the kill.

As they drew near the village Bolan took care not to leave evidence of their return. He picked his foot-steps carefully, urging Alna and Vanu to step only where he stepped. By so doing he hoped that Nevel, when he did find their trail, would not realise they had doubled back until he reached the river. The delay may gain them the time they desperately needed.

Eventually Bolan glimpsed the palisade through the trees and the sight urged him to hurry. But they had hardly gone 100 paces when they heard voices coming towards them. Nevel, or some of his men, must have found the coracle and were now following their trail.

Despite his alertness Bolan was taken by surprise. Panic gripped him and it was left to Alna to take evasive action. She thrust Vanu into the undergrowth and grabbed Bolan's arm, not daring to speak. Already the men were almost upon them.

Alna pulled Bolan with her into the undergrowth. There was no time to move further back and they crouched down where they were as the voices drew near. There was no mistaking Nevel's voice and that of Bador. They were in a good mood, laughing and joking as they approached.

'We've got them trapped,' Bador was saying. 'They won't escape us again. It's a pity they weren't on the other side of the river. Then the slaving party from Sarnay who stayed at the village last night might have caught them for us.'

'We'll have great sport hunting them down anyway,' another said.

'Bolan's mine,' Nevel warned. 'You can have the others.'

'We'll throw them in the river,' Bador said. 'That way they'll get to Sarnay much more quickly.' This drew a guffaw of laughter.

By now the children could see them clearly. There were four other men with Nevel and Bador. Bolan recognised them as the men who had gone with Faver on the hunt. They were armed with spears or axes. Two of them also carried bows and arrows.

They passed right by the spot where the children were concealed. Bolan was certain Nevel would sense their presence in the undergrowth. But he passed by without a glance. Soon he would reach the river and realise they had doubled back. They would be an angry and bloodthirsty group that returned this way. There would be no joking then.

'They'll kill us,' Vanu whispered. 'They'll throw us in the river.'

'No they won't,' Bolan said firmly. But he was only too aware that Vanu might be right. Could they hope to escape Nevel yet again? Surely their luck would run out. 'We must go on,' Bolan continued. 'We can still reach the boat and get across the river. We'll just have to keep a sharp look out for that raiding party from Sarnay.'

'Wait,' Alna said. 'Why are there only four men with Nevel and Bador?'

'He probably thought six of them were enough for the task,' Bolan said. 'And he would have left some behind to keep order at Marn.'

'Maybe,' Alna pondered. 'But don't you think he'd have left someone to guard the boat?'

Of course! Bolan knew she was right. Nevel would not have left the boat unguarded. He would not want to be made to look like a fool again. They could not go back. So what were they to do now?

The village seemed their last hope. There would be a bridge within the palisade. But how could they get inside? And more importantly, get safely back out again? Bolan wondered if there was a gate in this side of the palisade. If there was, they might be able to sneak in there. Somehow they had to cross the river and try and lose Nevel in the forest.

Like hunted animals Bolan led them towards the village. As they drew near the bare area outside the palisade he indicated to Alna and Vanu to remain in hiding while he stole forward to take a closer look.

At the edge of the bare area he crouched down. From here he could see the palisade clearly and immediately noted the massive gate. It was constructed of logs which seemed as substantial as the logs of the barrier itself. But what was most discouraging was that the gate was shut. There was no way they could sneak into the village.

Bolan was directly in line with the corner of the

palisade and could see the river where it emerged from the village. He was desperate now and ready to try anything that might help them escape Nevel. He wondered if he could cross there. If he could tie a rope to a log on either side of the river, then Alna and Vanu might be able to cross by clinging to it. He knew it would be dangerous, indeed foolhardy, but desperation drove him.

Making up his mind, he broke from cover. As he crossed the open ground he expected to hear a warning shout. But he reached the lee of the palisade without incident. The ground here was a quagmire and Bolan sank in the mud as he edged his way to the corner.

A little further away the river emerged from the village and Bolan was dismayed by the sight. Though hampered in its wild rush by the palisade, the current was still treacherously strong. Bitterly disappointed, Bolan stared at the seething water and then at the debris the river had deposited on the bank. There were bits of branches and brambles, and what looked like a leather garment. Also on the bank was a large blackened log.

Bolan was about to turn away when he realised the log could not have been swept down by the river. A log of its size would not have passed through the gaps in the palisade. He stared more intently, narrowing his eyes, and then scampered forward as quickly as the mud allowed. As he drew near he saw that it was not a log but an old dug out canoe.

It lay on its side, embedded in the mud, and obviously had not been used for a long time. Already it was rotting and when Bolan kicked at it a chunk broke away to reveal a yellow colour beneath. He kicked again at the spot but beneath the rotting surface the wood was firm. Bolan looked back at the water and then at the canoe. Time was running out. He had to make a decision now.

Almost before he realised it, he was running back to Alna and Vanu.

'We can cross the river,' he told them, concealing his doubts and fears. 'But we must hurry.'

There was no need to urge them and they gathered their belongings and followed Bolan at a run. They crossed the open area without mishap and Bolan led them to the canoe. Alna immediately looked scared but Bolan warned her with a shake of his head. Vanu was unaware of the danger and was excited at the prospect of going on the river once more.

The canoe was stuck fast and it took all their strength to prise it loose. They slithered about, falling a number of times, so when they eventually freed the canoe they were covered in mud from head to foot.

But they ignored this and rolled the canoe to the edge of the water. Once it was buoyant, Alna held it while Bolan placed their possessions inside.

Alna and Vanu now sat into the craft and Bolan climbed aboard. Even here, where the river had come up over the bank, he could feel the pull of the current. His plan was to sink the head of his axe in a log and use that to hold the canoe close to the palisade. Meanwhile, Alna and Vanu would push against the logs to propel the canoe forward. They would move from log to log until they reached the farther bank.

They negotiated the first few logs without a hitch. But as they moved farther out on the river the tug of the current increased. The strain on Bolan's arms was agonising. Twice they were almost swept away as Bolan changed the axe from one log to another. But they could not stop. They had to go on.

Almost one-third of the way across though Bolan had to halt. He needed to take a rest because now it was taking all of his strength to hold the canoe against the current. Gasping for breath, he held on tight to the handle of the axe, his cheek pressed against the log. Through the gap he could see the bridge and the village.

By the Assembly House a commotion caught his eye. Men were gathering there. A moment later a group of them headed for the east gate. They were led by Holt, a crony of Nevel's from Marn. Clearly Nevel had persuaded the villagers here to help with the search. He had probably told them that the children had committed some terrible crime.

Bolan knew they had to go on. But would they ever make it to the far bank? While he took deep breaths to prepare himself for the ordeal, their fate was already being decided, for just then a shout rang out.

It startled all three of them and Vanu jumped up in alarm. The canoe wobbled alarmingly and it took all Bolan's strength to hold it. But even as he held it he knew it was pointless. He did not need to look up to know that the man who had shouted a warning was on the far bank. They could not go forward. They were trapped.

There were two men on the far bank. Bolan recognised them as cronies of Nevel's. They were both brandishing spears and shouting to someone in the village. They were trying to alert Holt to the danger.

Bolan glanced into the village again. Already the east gate was open and the men were rushing through, urged on by the shouts. He turned again to look at the two men on the bank. He might be able to kill them both if he could reach them. But he knew now he would never make it to the other side. Even if he could beat the current, a spear would end his life before he reached the bank. Alna and Vanu would then be left to the fury of the river.

By now the group led by Holt reached the corner of the palisade and drew near the riverbank. They milled about and one of them took aim to throw a spear.

'No!' Holt shouted, grabbing the man's arm and preventing him from throwing the weapon. 'Nevel wants them alive. Go back to the village and bring a coracle. We'll go out there and get them.'

As two men ran off Nevel arrived on the scene with his group. Nevel said something when he saw the predicament his quarry was in which drew a burst of laughter from the group. Across the river the two men laughed too.

'What are we going to do, Bolan?' Alna asked.

Bolan did not answer. Instead he stared at the river, aware he had only two alternatives. Wait for Nevel's men to come and get them or give themselves up to the river. Either way seemed to spell certain death.

Already the men were returning with the coracle. Time was running out. Bolan's strength was waning. He would not be able to hold the canoe much longer. Like someone in a nightmare, he watched the men arrive with the coracle. It was quickly lowered into the water and Nevel and three others climbed aboard.

It was pushed out onto the river and two of the men began to row. Bolan made his decision. He released his grip on the axe.

Immediately the current took the canoe. But Bolan had had the presence of mind to push firmly against the palisade, thus turning the prow of the canoe downstream. If the current had caught it sideways on, it would have capsized, catapulting them into the water.

As the canoe shot forward, Nevel shouted. Bolan stole a glance back. Nevel was urging the men to pursue them, blind to the danger of the river. The men were clearly reluctant but Nevel forced them to comply at spear point. The coracle swung away from the shelter of the palisade and was taken by the current. It bobbed about on the water like a piece of wood. But with each thrust of the oars, it gained on the canoe. It seemed as if Nevel would capture them after all.

9

THE WILD RIVER RIDE

From time to time Bolan glanced back. He saw that the coracle was bobbing about on the water as if it were a leaf that had been blown into the river. But still it was gaining on them. Over another 100 paces Nevel would catch up with them.

Due to its sheer weight the canoe sat much lower in the water than the coracle. But despite this it too was at the mercy of the current. It was all the children could do to hold on tight, their hands gripping the edges of the craft made slippery from the slime and water.

Both craft were bobbing about so much that Bolan knew he would not be able to shoot an arrow with any accuracy. So there seemed little point in wasting them. When the coracle drew close he would use his spear to defend them. But he knew he could not fend off Nevel and his men forever. Eventually they would be taken.

As they sped on the current grew stronger, the water free now from the restriction of the palisade. The river ran straight here and Bolan saw the tributary that had blocked their passage ahead. It formed the left-hand prong of a giant leister. They were travelling on the other prong while up beyond the fork was the haft of the fishing spear.

At the junction of the two prongs the water was more turbulent and it swirled about as if enraged. The canoe had drifted on the current towards the far bank, away from the swirling water. But the coracle had not even made it to the centre of the river. The two oarsmen were paddling furiously, trying to force the craft further out on the river. But they were fighting a losing battle.

Nevel was no longer concentrating on the chase. He was urging the two oarsmen to even greater effort. However, the coracle, caught in the grip of the current, was being swept straight towards that swirling area of water.

The canoe passed the junction of the prongs and went on into the haft. Now Bolan stole another glance behind him. He was just in time to see the coracle caught by the whirlpool. It spun about crazily and water poured in over the sides. The occupants desperately tried to steady the boat, but it was hopeless. As it swung about, it almost capsized, flinging a man into the river. Bolan saw his hands claw at empty air, seeking something to grab on to. But there was nothing to save him and he disappeared beneath the water.

The coracle was doomed. Caught in the swirl of water, it would soon be swamped. But before that could happen it struck some unseen obstacle – a rock or part of a tree hidden beneath the surface. The small craft suddenly broke apart, giving its occupants up to the river.

Surely, Bolan thought, this was the end of Nevel and Bador? To his disbelief though he could still see them. Nevel, Bador and another man were clinging onto whatever the coracle had struck. Their lower bodies were submerged but Bolan could clearly see their shoulders, arms and heads. They were holding on tightly against the pull of the current. But they were strong men. They would survive until the villagers rescued them. For now they were out of the chase.

Bolan turned his head away from one danger to face another, for it was the river they now had to fear. They were hurtling along at what seemed breakneck speed, completely at the mercy of the current.

Even with oars they would not have been capable of fighting the river.

Bolan stared at either bank where the forest formed great barriers. It seemed to be part of another world – a world they might never enter again. He would have given anything for the security of the trees and would even have faced the wolves and bears. But there was no way of reaching the banks. The river held them prisoner.

He glanced back at Alna and Vanu, only becoming aware then that they were all covered in mud. From the expressions on their faces he knew they were terrified. For Vanu, this was no longer an adventure.

'We've lost Nevel,' Bolan said, trying to make his voice sound light and hopeful. But his fear showed in each word.

'Will we drown?' Vanu asked in a trembling voice.

Bolan shook his head vigorously.

'We will not drown,' he said firmly. 'Once we're well clear of Nevel we'll leave the river and make our way to Sarnay on foot. After we've washed off this mud. We can't let father see us like this.'

Vanu smiled bravely at his brother's words and Alna ruffled the little boy's hair. Bolan turned away with a lump in his throat, only too aware that they may never see their father again.

On they sped as the sun climbed higher in the sky. There was no cloud and it was growing warmer by the moment. The black water seemed to absorb the light, making the surface of the river murky and threatening.

There was much debris on the river. But it too was moving along on the current. At times they struck this debris, mostly branches of trees and bits of wood. At other times debris struck them. But with both objects in motion, the impacts were slight. What Bolan feared was an obstacle stuck firm in the water. If they struck one they were doomed.

Up ahead now the river swung sharply to the right. The current on the inside was moving slower than that on the outer reaches of the bend. The canoe was dragged towards the left bank as if by an invisible hand. It gathered speed and began to rock alarmingly from side to side.

There was nothing they could do. They simply had to hang on and hope the river was not intent on destroying them. They sped round the bend, narrowly avoiding a tree which had toppled into the water. And then up ahead, where the bank was devoid of trees, Bolan saw a nomad's camp.

The nomads were regarded as the enemies of the villagers. They lived a life that appeared irresponsible to the farmers. They hunted, fished and moved on, always restless to be elsewhere. His grandfather had told Bolan that their ancestors had been nomads too before they settled at Marn and began to practise agriculture and animal husbandry. He had also said that one day in the future the nomads would have to give up their way of life. The world was changing and they would have to change with it – it was either that or perish.

It was a village rule to avoid nomads. But Bolan realised this was not a time for rules. They could not escape the river by themselves. They needed help. Now, as they drew near the camp, a scattered collection of shelters made of animal skins, Bolan turned to the others.

'We must get help,' he said. 'I'll call out to the nomads to help us.'

'No!' It was Alna who spoke, the one word conveying her terror. 'They are to be feared, like Nevel.'

'But we must have help,' Bolan protested.

'No!' Alna spoke more vehemently. 'Better to drown,' she added, 'than to ... to ...' She couldn't put her fears into words.

Bolan hesitated. They were alongside the camp now. He could see men, women and children. They were preparing to eat and the thought of food made his stomach rumble. He opened his mouth to shout but held his tongue. And then one of the nomads spotted them and shouted a warning.

Suddenly everyone in the camp was turning to stare at them. They were only about twenty paces from the bank. They could clearly see the people. All were roughly dressed in animal skins. Their own skin was brown like leather from a life lived outdoors.

Now the camp became a hive of activity. Danger was a permanent part of their lives. Even a drifting canoe with three children might spell disaster. Women, children and older people hurried into the forest to hide. The men meanwhile grabbed their spears, bows and arrows and cautiously approached the water's edge.

Bolan knew they were within range of the weapons. He also knew that the nomads were deadly accurate. They had to be. Life or death could depend on a hunter hitting a fleeing animal with an arrow or spear.

Bolan expected spears and arrows to come streaking towards them. He tensed himself for the pain and shock of them penetrating his flesh – for that moment when he would know he was about to die. He stole a last glance back at Alna and Vanu. He was certain he would not see them alive again.

Their faces were animated with fear. He tried to

speak but before he could do so a shout rent the air. It caused him to stare at the nomads. One man stood ahead of the others. He was clearly the leader and was waving his bow in the air, shouting what seemed to be a warning.

Bolan did not catch the words. Only one stood out. Danger! Was it a warning or was the leader asking if they posed a danger? By now the current was taking them past the group on the bank. Soon they would be beyond the range of the weapons and Bolan began to feel relieved. But the relief was short lived. The leader and some of the men were running along the river-bank in pursuit. Bolan stared up river, seeking a means of escape. And only then did he become aware of a greater danger ahead.

He could hear it – the unmistakable roar of falling water. There was a waterfall not 1,000 paces ahead of them. They were heading straight towards it and would go hurtling over the edge to their doom. That was what the nomad's leader had tried to warn them about. He knew of the falls. He was on their side after all. At any other time Bolan would have been relieved to learn this. But not now. There was nothing the nomads could do.

Bolan glanced at the riverbank. Here again trees grew right up to the edge – alders, poplars and a few birches. They would hamper the nomad's progress. By the time they reached the falls the canoe would have long since gone over.

Alna and Vanu became aware of the new danger. Vanu began to whimper and Alna tried to soothe him. But her voice trembled with fear. Bolan wanted to cry out in desperation. But he was his father's son. Gaelan would never have given up while he had breath in his body.

Bolan stared ahead, seeking a way to save them. But there seemed to be none. And then he saw the tree. It was an alder which lay on its side in the river. It was directly in their path, half of its branches sticking out of the water.

'See the tree,' Bolan shouted, turning to Alna and Vanu. 'We must grab hold of it. It's our only chance. When the canoe comes in under the branches grab them and hang on. Keep your heads and we'll save ourselves yet.'

He turned back to see that they were almost upon the tree. Not far beyond it he could see the curling lip of the falls. The roar of the falling water was like thunder now. He saw the canoe was going to pass beneath the outer branches of the tree. There was no room for error. If they missed the tree then within moments they would go over the falls to oblivion.

As they came within reach of the tree Bolan stood

up and grabbed at a branch. Hanging on desperately, he tried to slow the canoe's progress with his feet to give Alna and Vanu a better chance. But the canoe kept on going. It broke off some smaller branches as it ploughed on and Bolan found himself hanging in mid air above the dark swirling water.

He managed to steal a glance backwards. To his relief both Alna and Vanu had also got hold of the branches. Now all three were hanging in mid air. There was no more time for observation though. Bolan had to save himself first. Slowly he hauled himself upwards until he hung over the branch which bent alarmingly under his weight. From beneath his eyebrows he watched the canoe go over the falls, taking all their weapons and supplies with it.

He carefully edged his way along the branch until it no longer bent beneath him. Now he could afford to look back to see how Alna and Vanu had fared. Alna had already reached a safe place. But Vanu seemed paralysed. He was unable to go forward. The branch he clung to was swaying alarmingly.

'Hang on, Vanu,' Bolan screamed. 'I'm coming to get you. Hang on!'

Sick with fear, Bolan clambered onto a nearby branch, edging closer to his brother. But Vanu's fear got the better of him. He looked down, saw the water and panicked. He tried to climb to safety but the branch began to sway all the more. Vanu lost his grip and fell. He screamed in terror just before he struck the water and as his head disappeared beneath the surface the scream died to a heart-chilling gurgle.

Alna screamed too. But Bolan kept his head. Oblivious to the danger, he dropped into the swirling water at the spot where Vanu had gone under. Everything seemed to happen in a split second. As Bolan hit the water and felt the pull of the current, Vanu bobbed up beside him. Bolan grabbed his brother's tunic in his left hand and with his right scrabbled for a branch directly above his head. His fingers closed about the branch which held firm. Already the current was trying to drag both Vanu and himself away, placing an almost intolerable strain on his arms.

It was Alna who saved them. She scrambled towards them with no thought for her own safely. Clambering onto an adjacent branch, she reached down for Vanu. She caught his tunic and took some of the strain off Bolan's arms. This allowed him to get a better grip on the branch. Together, they held onto Vanu and kept his head above the water. But they could not pull him up. If any more pressure were placed on either branch, they would break off.

Bolan and Alna could not hold on forever and

indeed all three were on the point of being swept away when the nomads arrived on the scene.

It was the leader who came out to them, a rope tied to his waist. He took Vanu in his arms and carried him to safety. He returned with a rope for both Alna and Bolan. Both were helped onto the riverbank, never before so relieved to feel solid ground beneath their feet.

10

THE NOMADS

The children were taken back to the nomad's camp. Kedo, the nomad's leader, a man of medium height with skin as brown and wrinkled as leather, carried Vanu in his arms. Bolan and Alna walked though they were exhausted from the ordeal. All three were soaked and Alna was still covered in mud. Their stomachs were rumbling but Bolan felt as though he would never want to eat again.

At the camp they became the centre of curiosity as all members of the tribe gathered to stare at them. Bolan was dejected, though glad to be alive. He had lost all their provisions and weapons. All he now possessed was his flint dagger.

Kedo ordered that they be taken care of. Dry

clothing and food were to be provided. When they had eaten they were to be brought to him. With that he strode away.

Some women took Bolan and Vanu to a shelter made from elk skins sewn together with animal sinews and propped up with timber poles. Here they were given dry clothing made from deerskin. Meanwhile Alna was taken to another shelter where she was able to wash off the mud and was also given dry clothing. The nomad women did not speak. Clearly they were as suspicious of the children as they in turn were suspicious of their benefactors.

When they were dry and comfortable they were taken along to the fire and given food. There were strips of roasted venison, tubers and fungi collected from the forest. The food was delicious and they ate their fill as their appetites returned.

While they ate the women and children gathered about them. There were fourteen women, both young and old, and nine children, the youngest of whom was but a baby held in its mother's arms. They all had dark complexions and thick black hair, and were dressed in deerskins. Many of the women and all of the children were barefoot.

When they had eaten a woman indicated they should come with her and they followed her to the edge of the camp where the men waited. Bolan knew they would have been discussing this odd happening and trying to decide what to do now. So far no threat had been made towards them. But if the nomads felt they posed a danger then there was no knowing what might happen.

Kedo squatted on the ground, the other men gathered about him. There were eleven in all. Only one of them was old, a man with long white hair who sat next to Kedo. The two youngest could hardly have been much older than Bolan himself. They all had weapons to hand. They were taking no chances.

Kedo ordered that Alna and Vanu be taken away. He would speak only with Bolan. Alna protested fearfully and clung to Bolan's arm while Vanu in turn clung to his sister.

'We will remain together,' Bolan said, staring at Kedo. 'We mean you no harm.' As if to demonstrate this, he held out his hands, showing his empty palms.

'I talk only with chief,' Kedo said firmly, determined to exert his authority. All the tribe had now drawn near and were watching. In this group the strongest was chief. But he had to be ready and willing to exert his power at all times as there were men like Nevel everywhere waiting for an opportunity to seize power for themselves.

Bolan realised their lives were in the hands of this man. If his authority was questioned he might kill them just to demonstrate to the tribe that he was not weak. So Bolan turned to Alna and Vanu, ordering them to do as they were told. He spoke in a commanding voice, wanting to show the nomads that he too was a leader. When they realised he was strong and determined, they would respect him all the more.

Alna and Vanu withdrew with the women and children. Bolan stretched to his full height and thrust out his chest. The nomads watched him and Bolan was certain they now had a new respect for him which he could use to his advantage.

'Sit.' Kedo indicated a spot on the ground opposite him where a piece of skin had been spread on the damp earth. Bolan sat, squatting down and crossing his legs. 'You must tell us where you come from,' Kedo said. 'And why you are here.' He pointed a finger at Bolan. 'Now.'

Bolan stared at Kedo, ignoring the others. It was this man who would decide their fate.

'I come a long way,' Bolan began, indicating the river and the forest beyond with a sweep of his hand, never once taking his eyes from the nomad. 'I am the son of a great chief, just like you.'

Kedo nodded, accepting the compliment, and

Bolan continued his story. He decided to tell the truth and he told of Nevel and his attempt to seize power. He told of how he had opposed Nevel and had escaped from the village, evading capture since. He emphasised in a strong and determined voice that when he was reunited with his father, they would crush Nevel.

Bolan explained that he himself did not fear Nevel. He would fight him and his men right now. But he had promised his father to take care of his sister and brother. He had to consider their safety. That was why he had run away with them.

A murmur went up from the nomads. Bravery and courage were things they understood. And they too had great concern for their families and knew the importance of children, for without children the tribe would die out.

'You are brave and courageous,' Kedo said now. He bowed to Bolan and the other men murmured again in agreement. 'We will help you. You must stay and rest with us. Tomorrow you can resume your journey to Sarnay. We know of the great settlement but we do not go near it. They use slaves to work the flint mines and the workshops. Many of the slaves are nomads like us. The Lord of Sarnay sends out raiding parties when he requires new slaves. We have to be on our guard against them at all times. Right now there is a raiding party in the area. That is why we were so suspicious of you.'

'We are peaceful people,' Bolan said. 'We do not have slaves at Marn. My father says that all people should live in peace.'

'He is a wise man,' Kedo said. 'Just like his son. Now we must leave you and prepare to hunt.'

Bolan rejoined Alna and Vanu. He told them that the nomads would help them. Both were overjoyed and now that Kedo had accepted them the other nomads did likewise. Vanu went off to play with the younger children and soon he was chasing about the clearing, hiding behind shelters, rocks and fallen trees. Alna went with two of the girls her own age to search for tubers and fruit in the forest. Bolan sought out Kedo and explained that he wanted to join them on the hunt.

Kedo agreed and Bolan was provided with a bow and arrows. The bow was made of yew and was per-fectly balanced. The arrows were expertly fletched with goose quill and would fly true. Four others from the tribe accompanied Kedo and Bolan. All carried bows and arrows while two also carried spears.

Kedo led the way, taking them deep into the forest until the sunlight was shut out by the umbrella of foliage. They were seeking wild boar and, from experience, the nomads knew exactly where the boar were to be found. Once they reached the immediate area they split up in order to encircle the prey. Bolan remained with Kedo while the others went off to left and right.

Moving stealthily now, hardly making a sound, Kedo led Bolan to the edge of a clearing. And there before them, in the middle of the clearing, stood a single wild boar. The well-fed animal, with its massive shoulders, was rooting in the ground. With a hand gesture, Kedo indicated to Bolan that they take cover in the undergrowth.

Silently they waited. Soon they heard a whistle from the far end of the clearing. Two more whistles sounded from either side. Kedo nodded at Bolan and whistled in reply. Now the beating could begin.

The four nomads burst from the forest on three sides of the clearing. The din they made gave the impression that there was a large group and not merely a handful. The startled boar stared about in panic and then bolted, taking the only apparent route to safety. With a speed that was surprising in such a cumbersome looking beast, it headed straight for the spot where Kedo and Bolan waited.

Both notched arrows to their bows and took a sight on the animal which was hurtling towards them. When the boar was hardly more than 30 paces away Kedo leaped up and yelled. The boar was startled by this unexpected development and halted in its headlong rush. It was the moment for Kedo to strike. His arrow sped true to its mark and buried itself in the animal's heart. The boar staggered and fell.

Even as the animal fell Kedo was moving towards it. He had ropes slung over his shoulder and he stooped now to tie the animal's fore and hind legs together so it could be slung on a pole and carried back to the camp.

It was then Bolan heard a roar behind him and a noise as some large animal charged through the forest. He swung about to see a wild aurochs burst from the edge of the trees. Something had driven it demented, perhaps the smell of blood on the air. Now maddened with fear, it charged straight at the spot where Kedo was tying the boar's legs together.

The latter had put down his bow and in desperation he grabbed for it. But he was too late. The aurochs, with head lowered and horns thrust wickedly forward, was bearing down on him at breakneck speed. The horns would rip him open and toss him away. He had only seconds to live.

It was Bolan who saved him. For a moment he had been paralysed by the suddenness of the event. But his father's advice that he never panic in such a situation stood him in good stead. He still had the arrow notched in his bow and now, as the aurochs bore down on Kedo, he took sight along the beast's neck which was covered with thick matted hair.

He could see the animal's eyes, maddened with fear and the smell of blood and death. He could hear its heavy breathing and its foetid stink carried to his nostrils. All this happened in the split second it took him to focus on that vital spot. If he missed the heart the impetus of the animal would carry it forward. Kedo could yet die.

Bolan held the goose quill flight to his cheek. He sighted along the arrow and made a slight adjustment for the movement of the aurochs. Then he released the arrow, urging it on with all his being.

His shot was true. The power of the yew bow delivered the sharp flint arrowhead to the precise spot. The arrow buried itself in the heart of the aurochs. But though it stumbled, its momentum kept it going forward. When it eventually fell it was but a few paces from Kedo, whose weathered face had become pale. He turned to Bolan and even before he spoke, Bolan saw the thanks in the eyes.

'We are even now,' Kedo said and turned back to continue tying the boar's feet.

Bolan shivered. Out here in the forest death could come at any time and in any guise. He thought of the journey still to come – of the dangers still to be faced. But he thrust the thought away as the rest of the nomads joined them. They were aware of what had happened but did not speak of it. They lived each day with danger. It was as much a part of their lives as eating or sleeping. But they treated Bolan with a new respect. He had not only proved himself as a man but as a great hunter. In their eyes he was now worthy of them.

11

THE NIGHT RAID

That evening a feast was prepared in Bolan's honour. Fires were lighted and the aroma of cooking meat wafted from the clay ovens. Bolan had a garland of owl feathers put about his neck as a sign of honour while Alna had flowers entwined in her hair. Meanwhile Vanu played with the children, his recent ordeals forgotten. Bolan watched him, relieved to see him happy again, and remembered his own childhood at Marn.

On long summer evenings such as this the people gathered outside the Assembly House or down by the river. While the men sat and talked, the women dangled their bare feet in the cool water. Bolan vividly remembered his own mother sitting on the bank, Alna just a baby then, held in her arms.

He had played with the younger children, paddling and splashing in the shallow water. But all the time he envied the older children who swam further out in the river or dived off the wooden bridge. He wanted so much to join them, to be a part of that exuberance.

From time to time he would look up at his mother, seeking her reassuring presence. She would smile and reach down to ruffle his hair and he in turn would splash water on her.

As the sun set and the river changed from a ribbon of dazzling light to one of darkness, they would make their way back to their homes. Bolan would ride on his father's shoulders, tired from the long day in the sun. Even as he was laid on his bed he would already be falling asleep, drifting off into a world of dreams where there was never any danger or threat.

Yet within just a few years everything had changed. With his mother's death, his childhood came to an end and his safe world was shattered. Responsibilities were thrust upon him but he was his father's son and he coped with them, just as he was coping now with the responsibility for Alna and Vanu's safety, and indeed his own. So far he had kept them alive. And when they were refreshed after a night's sleep they would be capable of continuing their journey.

A great fire was lit in the centre of the clearing. Here everyone gathered, eating, talking and laughing. Bolan sat in a place of honour between Kedo and the old white-haired nomad whose name was Jode. He was Kedo's father and had once been chief of the tribe.

As the flames lit up the faces of their new-found friends, Bolan felt safe for the first time since Nevel made his move for power. He began to relax and as the singing and dancing began, he forgot about Nevel altogether.

As darkness fell the singing and dancing became more boisterous. The children were the first to succumb to fatigue and were taken away to sleep. An extra shelter had been erected and Alna now took Vanu there. It had been placed at the edge of the clearing, close to the forest. It was well away from the fire and the noise of the festivities. Bolan intended leaving at dawn and did not want Vanu's sleep to be disrupted by the celebrations.

Eventually the fire burned down and the festivities came to an end. By now everyone was exhausted and looking forward to a night's rest. Bolan went to his shelter which had been pitched close to Jode's. Bolan took with him the bow he had used to kill the aurochs. It had been presented to him along with an axe and a spear to replace the ones he had lost. He had been told that the great aurochs horns would be used to make ornaments for the tribe. That way they would never forget his bravery.

Back at the shelter Bolan checked the weapons and the pouches of food and fresh water the nomads had also given them. Everything was now ready for the remainder of the journey to Sarnay.

Bolan lay on the soft bed of moss, grasses and herbs that had been prepared for him. He was still excited by the day's events and aware of how lucky they had been to find such good friends. Sleep was slow in coming and he lay awake, staring through a gap in the shelter at the night sky.

He wondered where Nevel might be right now. The nomads, who knew the countryside better than anyone, had told him that the village where they had lost Nevel was almost a day's travel away. But Bolan knew that if Nevel travelled all through the day then he would reach the camp here by nightfall.

He would not come near the camp or attack it. The nomads, who lived by hunting, by their expertise with bow, arrow and spear, were to be avoided at all costs. The villagers, many of whom no longer hunted or practised with their weapons, would be no match for the nomads.

For now Bolan knew they were safe. But tomorrow

they would have to leave the protection of their new-found friends. Nevel, if he survived the river, could not know where they were – indeed might assume they had drowned. But he would almost certainly carry out a search for them before coming to that conclusion.

With these thoughts swirling in his head, Bolan eventually slept. He dreamed of the day's events, the wild river ride jumbled up with scenes from the hunt. There was danger and a shout rent the air. He woke with a start, his heart thumping. At first he thought that the shout was part of his nightmare. Or that it was the cry of an animal in the forest.

But then the shout came again. This time there could be no mistaking the warning of danger. In an instant Bolan was on his feet, pulling aside the elk skin from which the shelter was made. It was still night but a light suffused the sky and he could see the other shelters scattered about the clearing. The camp was alive with movement but the figures Bolan could see were no more substantial than shadows.

Fear gripped Bolan and a tremor ran along his body, raising goose pimples on his skin. At Marn they had had the palisade to protect them from both man and animals. Here they were out in the open, without protection, except for wits and weapons.

Fear was as necessary for survival as food or heat. Ducking back into the shelter, he grabbed his spear and roused Alna and Vanu, alerting them to the danger in the night. The younger children were both numb with sleep but Bolan's urgency soon had then wide awake.

'What is it?' Alna asked, becoming aware that the camp was in turmoil.

'I don't know,' Bolan answered. 'Maybe it's an animal.'

'Or Nevel?' Alna's voice trembled.

'He'd never attack the camp with just a few men,' Bolan said, trying to convince himself. But he was aware that if Nevel was desperate enough he might have been driven to do so. Bolan stared out again just as someone lit a torch. It flared in the night and in its glaring light, Bolan saw the men who were attacking the camp. They were neither villagers nor nomads but big heavy men, well armed. Just then Bolan saw Nevel and Bador. They had captured Kedo and were holding him at spear point.

Anger gripped Bolan and he was tempted to charge across the clearing to Kedo's aid. But he realised it would have been pointless. There were too many enemies to face alone. Already they had rounded up most of the nomads, having caught them off guard. Men, women and children were being herded together. One or two men were giving orders and others were spreading out to search the extremities of the camp. Bolan knew that their only hope now was to flee.

Bolan scooped up two pouches containing provisions and thrust them into Alna's hands, along with his spear. Then he grabbed his bow and arrows and ducked back out of the shelter. Two men, shadowy figures in the dark, were coming straight towards them. They were hardly 50 paces away.

In one movement Bolan notched an arrow in his bowstring and fired. He had not taken aim and the arrow flew between the advancing figures. But it was enough to make them run for cover and gain Bolan valuable time.

He swung back to the shelter and then, close by, someone called his name. It was Jode.

'Over here,' Jode urged. 'Quickly now!' But Bolan did not need urging. He reached into the shelter and caught Vanu's arm, dragging him outside and back into the trees to where Jode waited. Alna followed in their wake.

'Follow me,' Jode whispered. 'Don't make any noise or speak. Quickly now. We haven't much time.' With that he turned and led them into the forest.

As they gained the shelter of the trees, shouts rang out behind them and a spear flew through the air, embedding itself in a tree close to where Jode had been crouching.

Vanu whimpered but Bolan gripped his arm tightly and the whimper died away. Jode led them on, twisting this way and that. Behind them they could hear the sound of pursuit as men blundered about in the undergrowth. At one time they heard men ahead of them to their right. Bolan's heart faltered but Jode did not hesitate. He swung to the left, knowing exactly where he was going.

Jode twisted this way and that until Bolan lost all sense of direction. But he noticed that the noise of pursuit was fading. Eventually it and the tumult from the camp faded altogether, and the night was still again except for the noise of the forest which never slept.

After some time Bolan noticed they were climbing. The ground was becoming progressively steeper. He thought of the strain this must cause Jode. But Jode was used to travelling and the years of his nomadic existence served him well.

Eventually Bolan noticed a change in the light surrounding them. They were emerging from the forest. They came out on a bare plateau and Jode stopped for the first time. The children gathered about him and could not help but note his harsh breathing. The exertion had been a trial for him.

'I've brought us here because this plateau is all rock,' Jode said. 'We'll leave no tracks for them to follow.'

'Who were those men who attacked the camp?' Bolan asked.

'Slavers.' Jode spat the word. 'From the raiding party in Sarnay.'

'But I saw Nevel and Bador were with them,' Bolan said.

'They must have met up with the slavers,' Jode said. 'Nevel must have agreed to help them in return for your capture.'

'They have taken your people,' Bolan said. 'But we're still free. Now we must help save your people from the mines. After all, you helped us.'

'But what can we do?' Jode asked. 'I am an old man and your sister and brother are only children. What can you do on your own?'

'I don't know,' Bolan said. 'But I did not save your son's life so that he could be enslaved.'

'You are brave,' Jode said. 'But there are many slavers. They are well armed and ruthless men. They do not place any value on human life. If you go against them they will kill or enslave you. What then of your responsibility to your brother and sister? And your father? Come. We must go on. Even if the slavers do not pursue us, Nevel will learn that you were in our camp and he will come seeking you.'

Bolan knew Jode was right. For the moment he must consider their own safety. But it was still with reluctance that he followed Jode across the plateau to where the forest began again. Jode led them back into the forest and after some time they came to the river. It was smaller than the river they had travelled on and already the flood waters were subsiding.

'This is the river I spoke of,' Jode said. 'It will lead us back on the trail to Sarnay. Many times I have come this way. Now I do so for the last time. When we reach the trail I will leave you.'

'You will come to Sarnay with us,' Bolan said firmly. 'There we'll plead with the Lord of Sarnay to release your people.'

Jode smiled. It was possible to see his features now as dawn lightened the sky. His face was wizened like a dried up tuber and beads of sweat stood out on his forehead despite the chill of the morning. But his dark eyes were still vibrant.

'I will never reach Sarnay,' he said quietly. 'But you must. You must find your father and warn him. He does not deserve to die when he has such brave and intelligent children.'

'We'll all go to Sarnay,' Bolan said. His voice sounded light but his heart was heavy. There was a certainty in Jode's words – a certainty and a sadness. It was as if he could see the future and knew he would not travel with them all the way.

'We must go on,' Bolan said now, taking charge. 'We'll eat later.'

Jode nodded. He waited until Bolan walked past to lead the way. Alna followed with Vanu and Jode brought up the rear. In single file they moved on, following the river, uncertain of what they faced.

But Bolan was ready to face what lay before them. It was the danger behind them that he feared. He was aware that Nevel might have recruited a tracker from the slavers. Or forced one of the nomads to work for him. At this very moment Nevel might be laughing at their foolishness.

12

THE JOURNEY CONTINUES

Through the summer morning they trundled on. But eventually Jode and Vanu began to suffer from the heat and exhaustion and Bolan called a halt. He shared out meagre rations of meat washed down with water. But afterwards they were still hungry.

Bolan knew they all needed to rest. But he was anxious to press on. Nevel was never far from his mind. So they continued, at times on Jode's instructions, leaving the river to take a short cut across country. Whenever they were in the open Bolan took the opportunity to look back for any sign of pursuit. But there was no sign of Nevel. Indeed not once did they see any sign of a human presence.

Bolan wondered if Nevel had given up the chase. Perhaps he had realised that his attempt to grab power had failed and he had joined the slavers, too frightened now to return to Marn. Was their ordeal already over? Bolan hoped so but until he knew for certain they would have to be cautious.

They stopped often for short rests and to eat a little meat and drink some water. But as evening drew in and the light began to fade, Bolan called a halt. They were all weak from hunger now and exhausted.

'We'll camp in this clearing for the night,' Bolan said. 'We must rest. Tomorrow will be another long arduous day. I'll go now and see if I can get us more meat. We'll have to eat it raw as we have no flints or tinder to light a fire.'

'I will light a fire,' Jode said. 'I've not forgotten the old ways. And there is plenty of firewood here.' He indicated a fallen tree near the edge of the clearing.

Bolan nodded and, taking his bow and arrows, left them. He headed for a spot by the river where he had seen evidence that deer came to drink. Once there he settled himself in the undergrowth to wait. Above the trees, the sky was suffused with a fierce red glow which gave the impression that the forest was on fire. Tomorrow would be another hot day.

Hunting at Marn had taught Bolan patience.

Waiting was the worst part of it. Once the animals appeared one's senses were heightened and everything was forgotten in the concentration required to pick out the one animal you decided to kill and then strike it true with an arrow.

All about him the daylight activities of the forest were winding down. Birds were flying back to the safety of the trees while deep within the forest itself, the creatures of the night were preparing for the hours of darkness. Across the stream Bolan saw a hare. It stood up on its hind legs and sniffed the air. Its ears pricked up and, with a bound, it disappeared into the undergrowth. It had heard something. A moment later Bolan heard it too. The deer were approaching.

They came tentatively into the open, alert for danger. They were led by a giant elk with wide spreading antlers. There were more than twenty in the herd, including the young. Bolan watched them, singling out a young doe. He was aware that no matter which one he killed, he would not be able to carry all the meat back to the camp.

The light was fading fast and he knew he should strike now. Anything might startle the animals and he would have little chance of a true hit if they stampeded. He nocked an arrow in his bowstring and took careful aim at his target. He loosed off the arrow and even as it left the bow he knew its aim was true.

The deer were alerted by the twang of the bow-string and the whoosh of the arrow through the air. They swung about in panic but the arrow was much swifter than their response. It hit its target and, as the other deer fled, the doe staggered about before keeling over at the edge of the water.

Even as the doe fell Bolan was on his feet and running towards the spot. He laid his bow on the ground and took out his knife. Normally the animal would be skinned but there was little point in doing that. The skin was of no use to him. What he wanted was meat.

With his knife he cut round the tops of the thighs, intending to sever the legs. He worked quickly, practise coming to his aid. He was glad that he had settled on a young animal for the flesh was tender. The bones proved difficult and it took much work and effort to separate the thigh bones from their sockets. But soon both back legs were severed from the body.

It was then Bolan heard the wolf. It bayed howled deep in the forest and was answered by others. Bolan shivered. Next to the bear, the wolf was the animal he feared most. Now that fear urged him on and he quickly washed his hands and knife in the river. Then he slung his bow across his shoulder and, carrying the two legs, hurried back to the camp.

Jode had lit a fire by rubbing two sticks together and the flames were a welcoming beacon to Bolan. The three were delighted to see him return and to see the meat. Bolan did not wish to dampen their spirits by mentioning the wolves. Instead he prepared the meat and soon the smell of cooking venison wafted on the evening air.

When the meat was cooked they ate until their stomachs were bloated. Bolan hung up the remaining meat on a branch out of the reach of predators. It would serve them the following day.

With their hunger sated, they sat round the fire while Jode reminisced about the past. He spoke of a time long ago when only nomads roamed the countryside, hunting for food as his tribe still did to this day. Then people came from across the seas bringing with them the idea of settlements, agriculture and domesticating animals. Many nomadic tribes copied this way of living as the groups grew too large for easy movement.

As villages grew up along the coast people moved inland. And as more and more people settled, the settlement at Sarnay, built around the flint mines there, grew larger. It was, according to stories Jode had heard, more than 100 times larger than any other village. From Sarnay traders moved out to the villages with flints, tools and pottery. Great boats came there from countries across the seas, bringing more settlers and new ideas. Soon, Jode explained, their nomadic way of life would be destroyed. As the forests disappeared, burned by the settlers in their quest for land to grow crops and raise animals, the places where they could hunt would become fewer. Soon all the forests would be gone.

'All?' Bolan said. 'But there is so much forest.'

Jode nodded. 'We'll not see it in my lifetime,' he said. 'Nor in your lifetime either. But one day your descendents will speak of a time when this country was covered in forest. They will speak of us nomadic people too but like the forest, our way of life will have disappeared too. We'll be farmers like you then, living in villages, raising animals instead of hunting them.'

'You must be sad,' Alna said, 'when you think of that.'

But Jode shook his head. 'I'm not sad,' he said. 'I'm old enough to know that the world is always changing. I've seen change during my lifetime and I know that change will keep happening. I'm an old man; I've lived far longer than most nomads. I've got my son and a grandson. I ...'

He stopped speaking suddenly and gazed into the dying fire. It was as if he had just remembered then that all his people had been taken by the slavers. They would never be free again. He was alone now – an old man with no one to care for him. Even if he survived the summer in the forest, the coming winter would kill him.

'You must come back to Marn with us,' Alna said, almost moved to tears at the plight of Jode. 'We'll take care of you there.'

'You must. You must.' Vanu grabbed the old man's arm. 'We won't let anything happen to you there.' Vanu's voice was breaking and large tears rolled down his cheeks.

'You are kind,' Jode said, pinching the boy's cheek. 'But with my people enslaved I do not wish to go on living. We are a free people. We owe allegiance to no one except to others of our tribe. We move about the country like the animals in the forest. There is no boundary for us. How can my people survive slavery? They will be caged and forced to work until they are of no more use. Then they will be killed.'

'Perhaps they will escape,' Bolan suggested. He too was saddened by the old man's plight and wanted to offer him some comfort.

'Perhaps,' Jode said. But there was little confidence in his voice. 'So few ever escape to tell stories of Sarnay – of its terrible cruelties.'

They grew silent as darkness descended like an animal skin drawn over the night sky. The skin was pricked with a myriad of holes and through them the light still peeped. All about them the forest was coming alive with the night-time's cacophony of predators and their prey.

'We should sleep now,' Jode said. 'Tomorrow we must travel on again. I must get you safely to Sarnay. Then my duty is done. Tomorrow we will enter territory that is the domain of the brown bear. We will have to be vigilant for the bear knows no fear. Against him we'll be like mice against a fox.'

Alna and Vanu shivered as they huddled on the ground, staying close to each other for comfort. Bolan watched them, aware that tomorrow they would have to face the unknown again. But before that they would have to survive this night. He stared into the darkness of the forest, sensing the presence of the wolves. There was danger everywhere – from Nevel behind them and the wolves all about and from the bears up ahead. For all he knew there may be no place left in which to seek sanctuary.

13

ENCOUNTER WITH WOLVES

Bolan could not relax. His mind was occupied with the wolves and the smell of venison. Right now the smell might be luring the wolves towards them, driving them into a frenzy. He reached out and touched his bow which was close by. But it did not give him any sense of protection. He knew that if the wolves attacked he would not be able to fight them off.

Bolan was determined to stay awake but eventually succumbed to fatigue. It was not a noise that later woke him but a feeling of menace. Instantly he became alert, his senses attuned for whatever spelt danger. He sat up listening and only noticed then that the forest seemed quieter. There was a stillness in the air. The moon was in its first phase and hung like a sickle blade above the trees. Soft light bathed the area in a gentle glow.

Bolan picked up his bow, careful not to make a sound. He stared into the darkness beyond the moonlight, seeking whatever it was threatened them. But there was nothing to be seen except the deep gloom. He sensed there was danger out there. He could feel it on the air like the smell of the venison. Had Nevel caught up with them? Had he been stalking them all along, aware of exactly where they were, quietly waiting his opportunity? Or was it the wolves that watched them from the darkness?

Bolan was about to alert the others when he glimpsed a flash of light among the trees. There could be no mistaking what it was – the glimmer of reflected moonlight from a wolf's eyes. It was slinking out towards them from the edge of the forest. Not just one wolf, Bolan knew, but a pack. They were almost certainly surrounded.

Bolan knew at any moment the wolf pack might attack. There was no time to lose. He gripped Jode's shoulder, waking him, the pressure of his fingers warning the old nomad that there was danger. Jode struggled to sit up, confused at being woken in the middle of the night.

'Wolves,' Bolan hissed.

Jode did not speak. Bolan saw him cock his head, listening. But there was nothing to hear.

'We're surrounded,' Bolan whispered. 'I've seen only one but there are others. I can sense their eyes on us.'

At that moment Alna woke. She sat up, rubbing the sleep from her eyes. Bolan warned her with a tap on the shoulder and she glanced about in panic, unable to see any danger but clearly aware of Bolan's fear. As she got up she disturbed Vanu and now he too woke. Bolan tried to warn him not to speak but was too late.

'What's wrong?' Vanu asked, his child's voice loud in the silence.

Before Bolan could answer, the silence was broken. Off to their left a wolf howled, a terrible baying sound that seemed to echo and re-echo about the forest. It was the leader who had howled and the remainder of the pack now answered him, baying like demented creatures, creating a circle of terror about the camp. With trembling fingers Bolan notched an arrow and stared out into the darkness, seeking a target.

'No!' Jode's warning shout rang out in the night, stilling Bolan. 'Do not draw blood. You'll drive them into a frenzy and then we'll be doomed. We must fight them with fire. It's the only thing they fear. Quickly now. We've no time to lose. They may attack at any moment.'

As he finished speaking, Jode scampered across to the remains of the fire. Without hesitation Bolan and Alna followed him. The fire was a heap of ashes and Jode, without thought for himself, thrust his hand into the heap, scattering the ashes about. A shower of sparks from some live embers beneath flew up into the night like a swarm of wasps, only to die in the darkness.

'There's some seed left,' Jode said. 'Gather wood from the dead tree while I fan the embers into life.'

Spurred by fear and the urgency in Jode's voice, Bolan and Alna ran to the dead tree. It was twenty paces from the fire, closer to the edge of the forest than Bolan would have wished. He sensed the presence of the wolves and was convinced that he could feel their foetid breath on his face. Anxiously scanning the deeper darkness at the edge of the trees for sight of them, he began to break branches from the tree trunk. The splintering of the dry wood seemed amplified 100 times in the deathly silence.

It must have disturbed the wolves because now Bolan heard a rustling noise in the undergrowth. Then they began to howl yet again. But instead of freezing him, he felt an adrenaline rush. Thrusting a bundle of branches at Alna he began feverishly to break off more.

Alna sprinted back and grabbed another bundle of wood. Bolan stole a glance over his shoulder and saw that the fire was burning now, silhouetting Jode against the backdrop of the forest. As a tongue of flame leaped high in the sky Bolan had a glimpse of the wolves. They had emerged from the trees and were slinking forward, ready to move in for the kill.

Before Bolan could cry out a warning, some sixth sense alerted Jode to the imminent danger. He grabbed a blazing branch from the fire and threw it at the wolves. Frightened by the flame, they yelped and drew back. Now they began to howl again, setting Bolan's teeth on edge. He could hear them pacing about behind him and it took all his will-power not to run for the fire.

It was blazing now and its promise of protection encouraged Bolan. He smashed off a number of large branches with his foot and Alna dragged them to the fire. There Vanu helped Jode feed the flames. They worked silently and feverishly until Jode called a halt.

'That's enough,' he shouted. 'Come and help me here.'

Bolan ran for the fire, dragging with him two more branches. The fire was burning fiercely now, the flames leaping the height of a man into the night. Jode was spreading out the burning wood, forming a circular barrier of fire.

'If they attack,' he instructed, 'grab a blazing piece of wood to defend yourself. It's our only hope.'

They nodded and now began to help Jode build the circle. But before it was complete the wolves attacked. It was as if they had sensed that once the circle was made they would have no chance. They slunk in close at the point where the circle was incomplete and suddenly the leader sprang.

Jode's advice stood them in good stead. They grabbed pieces of flaming wood from the fire and thrust them at the wolf. He was almost upon them. He was so close they saw his yellow eyes and savage teeth, and the drool of saliva from his gaping jaws before he twisted away from the burning wood. But he was not quick enough and flames licked his snout. There was a stench of charred hair and flesh and a yelp of agony as the animal dashed back into the safety of the darkness.

The pack began to howl yet again. Their baying rent the night, creating a circle of terror about the camp.

'If they're going to attack, they'll do so now,' Jode warned. 'Be prepared.'

They all four grabbed fresh brands from the fire. They continued staring into the night, expectant, waiting for the attack that might be the final, fatal one. But the wolves did not draw near again. They were still there, their eyes glowing bright in the firelight. But without a leader, they were in disarray.

'They've had enough for now,' Jode said. 'So help me finish off the circle.'

They completed the circle and huddled together within it. They fed the fire as the night passed, keeping the protective circle intact. Jode kept their spirits up with stories of his adventures. He assured them that they would be safe and that the wolves would be gone by morning.

In this he was proved correct. When dawn did come the wolves had gone. The fire had almost died out and they sat in the circle of embers to eat some of the venison. It was simply food and they did not relish it. They were only too aware that they themselves had almost been food for the wolves just hours before.

When they had eaten they took the remainder of the meat with them and set off once more. They were chastened by the night's experience and did not even want to talk about it. Bolan led them on in silence, each oblivious to his surroundings, concentrating simply on advancing on their journey.

They were exhausted from their ordeal and by lack of sleep and rest, so much so that no one considered the possibility that today they might encounter a much deadlier enemy. As Jode had pointed out last night, they were now entering the territory of the brown bear.

14

THE BROWN BEAR

They walked through the morning, following the course of the river. At times it meandered through the forest; other times it traversed great tracts of open countryside. At noon they stopped to eat, glad of the respite. Not used to such walking, their feet were beginning to blister and they were relieved to have the opportunity to dangle them in the cool water.

The floods had subsided by now and the water sang and sparkled as it tumbled over the stones on its way to the sea. The river teemed with trout and they darted hither and thither, their movement quicker than the human eye. One brushed Vanu's toes and he squealed with half pleasure and half fear.

'They'll nibble your toes,' Alna laughed, cuffing

Vanu playfully. But just then a trout brushed her own toes and she leapt up, squealing louder than Vanu had. They all laughed at this, even Alna joining in when she saw the funny side of it.

When they had eaten Bolan allowed them to rest for a little while. But he himself could not relax. He wanted to be moving on.

'How far is it from here to the ferry?' he asked Jode.

'We should reach the ferry by evening,' Jode said. 'It's a day's walk from there to Sarnay.'

As he spoke the name aloud it brought a tightness to his features. Clearly he was still occupied with thoughts of his son, his grandson and his people. Bolan wished he could help him. But how could he save the nomads from their fate? He could never oppose the Lord of Sarnay. His power was absolute. If a threat were made against him, he would crush the village of Marn and enslave everyone there.

Bolan kept these thoughts to himself.

'We'll try and reach the ferry by nightfall,' Bolan suggested. 'We can camp close by overnight. Then tomorrow in daylight we'll travel the remainder of the way to Sarnay. So we'd best get moving again if we want to reach the ferry before dark.'

No one objected to this and they rose and plodded

on, fatigue making every step an effort. Towards evening they emerged from the forest into a small clearing. And as they stood to survey the landscape, they saw the bear.

It emerged from the trees on the far side of the clearing, a sight to strike terror into even the bravest heart. The animal stood up on its rear legs, its long snout sniffing the wind for any scent of danger.

'It's a she-bear,' Jode whispered. 'At this time of year it almost certainly has a den nearby and is raising cubs. A mother bear with cubs is doubly dangerous.'

Bolan nodded, staring transfixed at the giant animal. It was almost twice the height of a man and must have weighed as much as eight men put together. The bear was the supreme ruler of the forest, feared by all. Even a sick or injured bear was to be avoided.

They watched it now as it stood surveying all about it. Satisfied with what it saw or smelled, it dropped on all fours and lumbered clumsily along the edge of the trees. But the watchers were not fooled by that lumbering gait. In an instant it could change to a run, still clumsy and lumbering perhaps, but absolutely lethal. Nothing or no one could withstand it. It could cleave a man open from head to foot with one swipe of those great forepaws. Or failing that, its jaws, with their two rows of fearsome teeth, could crush a man's body as easily as a hunting dog might crush the body of a hare.

Jode held up a hand for silence while they watched the animal lumber back into the trees and disappear. Only now did he turn to the others, his face grim.

'It's said that a bear can hear the beat of a butter-fly's wings at 100 paces,' he said. 'Or smell a man on the wind at 1,000 paces. We're lucky the wind is blowing towards us. Otherwise we might be fleeing for our lives right now. Not that fleeing would do us any good. A bear can run for days without food or water. We could never avoid it.'

'We should push on,' Bolan said. 'It's much too dangerous here. Maybe when we reach the ferry we can cross the river before nightfall.'

Jode nodded. 'We are close to the ferry now,' he agreed. 'It might be best to have the river between you and the bear. I will see you safely across and then I must leave you.'

'You intend to leave us then?' Bolan asked.

Jode nodded. 'I must try to find my own kind,' he said.

'You could come back to Marn with us,' Alna said. 'We would take care of you.'

Jode smiled. 'I know you would,' he said. 'But I'm an old man. I want to be with my own people. I want to die with them.'

The mention of death brought gloom upon them. But Jode shook them out of it.

'Come,' he said. 'We must go on.'

'What if there are bears on the other side of the river?' Vanu asked in a tremulous voice.

'Of course there aren't bears on the other side of the river,' Jode assured the child. But the others could tell from his tone of voice that he was not speaking the truth. 'Even if there was a bear, your brave brother would not let it harm you,' Jode continued. 'He will keep you safe.'

With that they set off once more, Jode's words hanging like heavy weights from Bolan's shoulders. Soon they would be on their own again and he would have sole responsibility for all their safety. He wished Jode could have accompanied them to Sarnay. He had come to rely on the old nomad and to feel for him the affection he had once had for his grandfather.

The light was slanting through the trees when Jode called a halt.

'We are almost there,' he said. 'We must be careful from now on.'

Bolan nodded and led the way forward, even more vigilant now, if that was possible. The first warning he had that they were close to the trail was when he heard the sound of running water. The Ohan River was just ahead, the trail leading to the ferry running beside it.

Bolan and Jode proceeded and came upon the trail. It had almost dried out after the rain and they could see evidence in the mud that a large party had passed here quite recently.

'Almost certainly the slavers with my people,' Jode said, and looked wistfully along the trail towards Sarnay. 'There's nothing we can do for them now.'

Bolan did not speak. He was saddened at the thought of not being able to help Jode and the nomads. After all, they owed their lives to them. If only they could have rescued the nomads from the slavers. But what could they do against so many? And he had his father, Alna and Vanu to consider. They were all still in great danger.

Bolan wondered where Nevel and Bador might be. Had they remained with the slavers or not? If they had, then they might have reached Sarnay already and killed Gaelan? If they had done so then they could safely go back to Marn knowing Bolan and the others could not return there. Nevel would leave them to the forest, aware they could not hope to survive forever. If the slavers did not get them then the wolves would.

These thoughts made Bolan anxious to press on

and he returned to where Alna and Vanu waited. He led them back to Jode. They were about to move out onto the trail when they heard men approaching. Quickly they ducked back into the shadows of the trees.

They were just in time, for a small group of men came along the trail. There were six slavers, dressed in their rough garb of animal skins. All were heavily armed. With them were three nomads walking in single file, their heads hanging down. They were linked together with ropes. About each man's neck hung a heavy piece of wood which struck against his knees as he walked, preventing him from having ease of movement.

The leading nomad had a halter about his neck and was being led by one of the slavers. The slaver kept jerking on the halter, causing the nomad to stumble forward. One particularly vicious jerk brought the nomad to his knees. He was pulled back up by the slaver with the halter while two others kicked him mercilessly.

'We'll teach you a lesson you won't forget,' one of them growled. 'You'll think twice before trying to escape again.'

At this a third slaver intervened, striking out at his companions.

'Do you want to kill him before we reach Sarnay?'

he roared. 'He's no good to us dead. The Lord of Sarnay does not pay for dead men.'

The party moved on again and now the leading nomad raised his head. The watchers, who crouched at the side of the trail, gasped, for they saw that the prisoner was Kedo. Bolan, aware of the danger they faced, gripped Jode's arm, the pressure of his fingers warning him not to cry out. In silence they watched the group pass by the spot where they were hiding.

They could see Kedo clearly now. He was clearly suffering from fatigue and ill treatment. His face and body were badly bruised and stained red with his blood. Both his knees were chaffed from the constant blows of the wooden restraint.

The group passed by and only when they were out of earshot did Bolan speak.

'We must do something,' he urged. 'We cannot leave Kedo and the other two to their fate.'

'But what can we do?' Jode asked, his voice almost breaking.

'We must try and rescue them,' Alna suggested. Her eyes were wide with pity for the imprisoned men. They had helped to save them when they were in great danger and had treated them with hospitality. It did not seem right now to ignore their sorry plight.

'Kedo and his two companions must have escaped,'

Bolan said. 'Those six were sent to find them and bring them back. The rest must have continued on to Sarnay. So there are only the six slavers guarding the prisoners. They cannot reach Sarnay today. That means they'll have to camp along the trail tonight. They'll not be expecting danger so close to the settlement. So if we wait until they have settled down for the night, maybe we can sneak into the camp and free Kedo and his companions.'

'It would be dangerous for you all,' Jode said, but his warning words could not hide the hope in his voice. They could see he was broken by what he had seen. Kedo was his only son. How could he bear to see him suffer or leave him to his terrible fate?

'There will be some danger,' Bolan said. 'But we'll have the element of surprise and the darkness on our side.'

'We must do it,' Alna said. 'We owe the nomads that much.'

'You might succeed,' Jode said. 'But you must promise me that you'll not put yourselves in any danger.'

They agreed and Bolan led them back onto the trail. He had decided he should scout ahead for danger. If he gave a warning signal they were to duck back into the forest immediately.

Bolan moved forward quickly but stealthily. He

soon caught sight of the group ahead and made sure he remained well behind them. He did not want to give them any warning that they were being followed, for any hope of freeing the nomads depended entirely on the element of surprise.

The light slowly faded and it was almost dark when Bolan spotted smoke from a fire up ahead. He grew more cautious and as he approached the spot he smelled meat cooking. He stole forward and rounded a bend in the trail. Up ahead he saw the slavers join with others of their kind. Now there were at least twelve slavers in the camp. Beyond them he could see the ferry.

Bolan drew close, keeping under cover. He saw the three nomads huddled at the edge of the trail. They were still roped together. The slavers had gathered about the fire on which a young boar was being roasted on a spit. Bolan's mouth watered at the aroma of the roasting meat. And then fear dried up the saliva, for there at the fire sat Nevel and Bador.

With a sinking feeling Bolan knew he had been outwitted. Nevel had clearly learned from the nomads that Jode would have to lead them here if they were to reach Sarnay. So rather than pursue them across alien country, Nevel had simply gone along the trail with the slavers and had waited here for them. That explained why there had been no pursuit.

Bolan withdrew and made his way back to where the others waited and told them of what he'd seen.

'Nevel will be keeping a watchful eye on the trail for you,' Jode said, his voice filled with resignation. 'He'll almost certainly have a guard posted. You'll not be able to sneak into the camp now. So you must slip past there tonight. Nevel's no fool. He'll expect you to reach here by tomorrow. If you don't he'll seek you out. By then you must be well on your way to Sarnay.'

'But what about Kedo?' Alna said. 'And the other two?'

'They are doomed,' Jode sighed. 'There's nothing we can do for them now. You must save yourselves. I will see you safely past the camp. Then I'll seek out my own people as I'd originally planned.'

They waited for darkness and then moved stealthily through the forest, giving the camp a wide berth. But just when they thought they were safely past, disaster struck.

Jode almost saved them. Some sixth sense warned him of the trap which had almost certainly been set by the slavers. It consisted of a counter weight tied to the end of a rope and hoisted on a tree high into the air. The other end of the rope formed a loop on the ground. A trigger consisting of a bent piece of supple wood sprang the trap.

Jode called out a warning but he was too late. Vanu stood on the trigger and the trap was sprung. As the counter weight plummeted down, the loop of rope spread out on the ground whipped tightly about Vanu's leg. As he screamed in terror he was yanked up into the air by the ankle. Dangling high above the ground he continued to scream, rousing the slaver's camp.

Their shouts and yells of alarm rent the night as they were alerted to the danger. Bolan and Alna were paralysed with fear, hardly able to move. Jode grabbed Bolan's arm and tried to drag him away.

'No,' Bolan screamed. 'I can't leave Vanu.'

'You can't help Vanu right now,' Jode hissed. 'And you must not let Nevel capture you too. If you're all caught Nevel will kill you straightaway. But he will not kill Vanu just now. He will use him as a bargaining tool to make you give yourselves up.'

'He will kill us then,' Bolan said.

'But you'll have some hope of saving Vanu while you're free,' Jode said. 'If you give yourself up you're all doomed.'

Bolan hesitated. Above his head the helpless Vanu still screamed with terror. Further back in the trees the slavers were heading towards them. He could see the glow of the torches they carried. He had to make a decision now. Seconds counted. He looked at Alna and in the gloom he saw the fear in her eyes. But there was courage there too and determination. He knew Jode was right in what he said. If they gave themselves up to Nevel now he would kill them all.

Bolan hesitated no longer. Calling to Vanu that he would not leave him to his fate he melted away with Alna and Jode into the cover of the forest. As quickly and as silently as possible, they fled from the spot, leaving Vanu at the mercy of Nevel.

As they fled they heard Nevel shout after them. 'Come back and give yourselves up,' he roared. 'You've got until morning, Bolan. Then I'll kill Vanu and come and hunt you down. I know where you are and you will not escape me again.'

But Bolan did not stop. Instead he concentrated on putting as much distance between himself and Nevel as possible. In his mind the threat loomed large and forbidding though. After so much danger, it seemed as if Nevel would win in the end.

15

A RESCUE PLAN

When he felt they were safe from pursuit, Bolan stopped his headlong flight. They were deep in the forest now, Vanu's screams of terror no longer audible. Bolan and Alna were breathing heavily from fear and exertion, while Jode's breath came in short gasps and he had to cling to a tree for support.

'We must keep running,' Alna gasped. 'Or Nevel will find us.'

'He doesn't need to find us,' Bolan said. 'He knows that his threat to kill Vanu will force us to give ourselves up. Which is what we must do. If Vanu is to die, then we must die together.'

At this Alna fell silent. The thought of giving

herself up to Nevel terrified her. But to think of Vanu at the mercy of the slavers ...

'We must give ourselves up right away,' she said. 'We cannot leave Vanu alone with those terrible men.'

'He'll come to no harm for now,' Bolan assured his sister. 'While he's alive he's of use to Nevel. But if we don't give ourselves up by morning Nevel will kill Vanu and come and find us.'

At this pronouncement silence descended on the group, except for Jode's harsh breathing. They were all tired, hungry and dispirited. They seemed doomed to failure so close to the end of their journey.

Bolan did not want to succumb to failure and he considered the possibility of rescuing Vanu. But he could not see how it could be achieved. He might be able to creep into the slaver's camp – after all, Nevel would never dream of him attempting such a thing. But he would have to find Vanu and free him, and get back out safely. Even then they would not escape. Nevel would guard the trail to Sarnay and mercilessly hunt them down.

Despite this Bolan knew he could not leave Vanu to his fate, nor meekly give himself and Alna up to Nevel.

Alna became aware of Jode's harsh breathing and approached the old man.

'Sit down, Jode,' she said, taking his arm. Bolan

came to her aid and they helped Jode to sit with his back to the tree.

'I'm too old for this,' he said, between his gasps for breath. 'I can't go on much longer.'

'Of course you can,' Bolan said, a lump rising in his throat.

'You're a good lad, Bolan,' Jode said. 'Your father must be very proud of you. But my day has come. Only I don't want to die sitting here among the trees. So I'm going to give you a chance to save your brother and my son from the slavers. Now sit down here and listen carefully.'

Jode outlined a plan and at first Bolan and Alna tried to dissuade him from it. But the old nomad was stubborn.

'I won't see the autumn,' he said. 'So isn't it better to die a brave man than to wait for death to catch up with me? We won't argue about it any more. I'm just wasting precious breath. Now, let's go over the details one more time. And don't forget. Once the alarm is raised you must get onto the ferry. The wind favours you and if the spirits are with you they'll keep you safe. There's no time to lose. As I said, I'm an old man and not as nimble as I used to be.'

Bolan and Alna hung their heads in silence. They knew Jode was giving them a chance to save themselves. But if his plan succeeded, he would certainly die.

Jode seemed imbued with energy and a great sense of urgency. Since he had come to his decision to act he seemed to have become young again. He was no longer breathing heavily and he got to his feet with ease.

'Come,' he said. 'We've no time to lose.'

Bolan and Alna now rose reluctantly. Jode gripped one of their arms in each of his hands.

'We will succeed,' he said. 'And do not worry about me. I feel like a young man again on the threshold of life. Now go.'

They were about to speak but Jode gripped their arms even tighter and they remained silent. He then released them and thrust them away. They began to walk away from him and then, impulsively, Alna turned back and threw her arms about the old nomad's neck and hugged him close. Then she broke away and, joining Bolan, they began to run back towards the slaver's camp.

As they drew near they moved more cautiously. Through the trees they glimpsed the flames of the fire and, using it as a guide, they skirted the camp. Bolan led the way, crossing the trail and slipping back into the forest on the other side. When he had last seen Kedo and the other two nomads they had been tied together with their backs to the forest. He was hoping Vanu was tied up with them.

Bolan hoped to creep up on them from the forest and cut their bonds, leaving them free to run when he gave the signal. But if Vanu were being held elsewhere, then that would make his task all the more dangerous, for he would have to find Vanu and free his bonds too before Jode brought terror and death down on the camp.

Again, using the fire as a guide, Bolan and Alna moved like shadows through the trees until they were directly behind the nomads. Then, being extra careful not to betray themselves, they crept towards the camp. Bolan counted twelve men gathered about the fire. He could see them against the flames which leaped high in the air. Narrowing his eyes, he sought out the shadowy figures of the nomads. He looked for Vanu but could not see him.

'I can't see Vanu,' Alna whispered. 'Maybe Nevel has killed him.'

'No!' Bolan whispered vehemently in turn, gripping her arm. 'Now you wait here. I'm going to move in closer.'

'Be careful,' Alna warned, terror stricken at the thought of finding herself alone in the forest at the mercy of predators and the slavers.

'You'll be fine,' Bolan assured her. 'I'll leave my weapons here. They would only get in my way.'

With that he crept forward towards the camp. He picked his steps with care, making slow but certain progress. And, when he was quite close to the nomads, Bolan stood on a piece of a dry twig. It broke with a very loud crack, alerting the slavers to danger. They leapt to their feet, grabbing their weapons, instantly prepared for whatever threat faced them.

They began to argue among themselves. Some advocated going to see what had made the noise. But some others did not want to leave the fire. They were well aware the forest was dangerous at night.

'Check the captives,' a young man ordered now. He seemed to be the youngest of the party, yet his voice rang out authoritatively. He was taller than the slavers and unlike them, had blond hair. He was dressed in a lynx skin jacket and beaver leggings and a large amulet hung about his neck.

One of the slavers hesitantly approached the nomads, his spear at the ready. At the edge of the trail he stood and stared out into the darkness, seemingly straight at the spot where Bolan crouched down. He tried to shrink even lower still and realised that he could not be seen. The slaver checked the nomads and after kicking Kedo, moved back to the fire. Here they all sat down again and Bolan breathed a sigh of relief.

After giving the slavers time to re-settle, Bolan crawled forward until he came up behind Kedo.

'Don't turn round,' Bolan whispered. 'The slavers may be watching. Now I'm going to cut your bonds. But you must remain here and pretend to still be tied up. Don't do anything until I give a signal. It will be three owl hoots. When you hear it make for the ferry. Don't hesitate or all will be lost. Do you understand?'

Kedo nodded as Bolan cut through the ropes tying his wrists and then the rope from which the wooden restraint hung about his neck. Lastly he cut the rope binding Kedo to the next nomad in line.

'Do you know where Vanu is?' Bolan asked.

'At the end of the line,' Kedo whispered.

Bolan touched Kedo's arm to acknowledge his reply and moved on to the next nomad. He cut this man's bonds and then the bonds of the third nomad. As he did so, he saw Vanu. He was curled up in a ball, his hands and feet bound together.

Bolan felt a surge of anger but fought it. He crawled along to where Vanu lay and gripped his brother's shoulder, digging in his fingers as a warning. Vanu realised who it was and remained silent. He too was aware of the gravity of the situation.

'I've come to free you,' Bolan whispered. 'I'm going to cut the ropes tying your wrists and legs. But you mustn't move yet. The slavers must not know that you're free. Do you understand?'

Vanu nodded. 'It won't be long now,' Bolan said. 'I'm going back into the forest. When I call your name come straight to me. Now you must be very brave.'

His task complete for now, Bolan crept back to Alna. 'They're free,' he told her. 'Vanu's fine. He'll soon be with us again. We've only got to wait now for Jode.'

While they waited the fire died down and the slavers began to prepare for their night's sleep. One man was put on guard. But before the slavers could actually settle down, Jode's voice came out of the darkness beyond the camp.

'Nevel,' he called. 'Nevel. I want to talk with you.'

The slavers were alerted by the voice and for a second time they leapt to their feet, grabbing their weapons.

'Nevel.' Jode spoke again. The name rang out authorititively in the night. 'I have come to bargain with you. My name is Jode. I am one of the nomads. You have my son Kedo. In return for his freedom I will lead you to the two children you seek.'

'Why would you do that?' Nevel asked, as the young leader gesticulated to the others to spread out. Bunched together they made a perfect target for a bowman in the trees.

'I am an old man,' Jode said. 'I am all alone since

you took my people and my son. I need my son to take care of me. In return for his freedom I will lead you to the children. They are sleeping nearby. You will be able to take them without any trouble.'

'How can I trust you?' Nevel asked.

'What can an old man do to you?' Jode asked. 'But if you are afraid ...'

The jibe got through to Nevel. He did not want to appear cowardly to the slavers who knew no fear.

'I agree to your demand,' Nevel said. 'When the children have been captured I'll let Kedo go free.'

'I accept,' Jode said. 'Now come with me and I'll take you to the place where they sleep.'

From the cover of the trees Bolan and Alna saw Nevel and Bador, along with the leader of the slavers and five others, leave the camp and go towards where Jode waited. Bolan knew Nevel lied when he promised to free Kedo. If Jode had been really betraying them, Nevel would simply kill the old man once he and Alna were taken. Jode would be of little use as a slave. He would not last two days in the harsh regime at Sarnay.

As the party left the camp the remaining slavers settled down by the fire. No one would sleep again until their companions returned with the captives. Bolan and Alna waited too, tense with expectation.

Would Nevel realise it was a trick before Jode could put his plan into action? If this happened Nevel would kill the old nomad and return here with vengeance in his heart.

Bolan intended to be ready. If he had any inkling that the plan had gone wrong he would give the signal anyway and hope for the best. If he did not do so, Nevel would kill Vanu and in the morning would seek out Alna and himself. And it would not take him long to find them.

16

TERROR STRIKES

As time dragged on Bolan began to think the plan had failed. But as he was about to give up hope he heard screams ring out deep in the forest. They were blood curdling, drawn out screams of terror and agony and they raised goose pimples on Bolan's skin. They alerted the camp, causing panic among the slavers who milled about the fire, seeking a danger they could not see.

Again the screams rent the night, making hair stand on end and blood run cold in veins. They seemed to drown out all the other noises of the forest. And then another noise could be heard – the unmistakable sound of a great creature smashing its way through the forest towards the camp.

As the first screams rang out Bolan was on his feet, an arrow notched in his bow.

'Vanu,' he called. 'Vanu!' He fired the arrow into the group of slavers by the fire and heard a grunt of pain as the arrow struck home. From the corner of his eye he saw Vanu leap to his feet and come running towards him. Bolan notched another arrow and as he fired he gave the signal of three owl hoots to the nomads.

At the signal Kedo and the other nomads leapt to their feet, screaming like demons. It was all too much for the slavers. Danger seemed all about them. From behind they were being attacked with arrows. In their midst the nomads, whom they had thought were securely bound, were also attacking them. And from up ahead came that terrible sound which could only mean one thing. A great bear, the most feared creature on the earth, was rushing straight towards them.

Bolan fired no more arrows. He was frightened he would hit one of the nomads who, instead of fleeing for the ferry, were attacking the slavers with their bare hands. Kedo had grabbed a brand from the fire and was using it as a club to drive the slavers back.

The sound of the approaching bear was now like thunder as it smashed its way through the forest. Bolan knew time was running out.

'Get Vanu and run for the ferry,' he ordered Alna. 'Wait for me there.'

'But what about you?' Alna asked.

'I can't leave Kedo and the others at the mercy of the slavers.' Bolan said. 'Now go.'

As he spoke Vanu reached them. Bolan grabbed his brother's arm and thrust him at Alna.

'Go!' he screamed and the force of his voice made Alna obey.

Bolan gave the owl hoot signal again and notched another arrow, seeking a target. But by now the slavers were only interested in saving themselves. With danger seemingly on all sides, they began to run back towards Marn, leaving the man Bolan had injured to hobble after them, calling for mercy.

Kedo and the other nomads left them be and ran to join Bolan.

'Where's my father?' Kedo demanded. 'I cannot leave him.'

'You cannot go back,' Bolan shouted. 'Jode knew what he was doing. He wanted it this way. He's given us a chance to live. If you don't come with me, then the bear will kill you.'

Kedo hesitated. Already the bear was almost upon them. The ground vibrated beneath their feet as the enraged animal pounded his way through the trees.

'You're right,' Kedo said. 'There is nothing we can do here. I must do as my father wished. Quickly. There's no time to lose.'

As if they needed urging, just then the bear burst into the camp. It reared up on its hind legs, driven demented by the threat to its cubs and the smell of blood and of man. Its great jaws were wide open, showing the rows of fearsome teeth, and it roared with rage and defiance.

For a moment the fire halted it, striking fear in its heart. But then it spotted the injured slaver or else smelled his blood. With a swiftness of movement that belied its clumsy bulk, the bear bore down on the slaver. A great forepaw struck out at the fleeing man, sending him flying through the air. His scream of terror and agony died out in a gurgle as the bear crushed him beneath its massive hind paws.

The animal did not hesitate in its run but continued on in pursuit of the other slavers. And as Bolan and the nomads ran for the ferry, they heard another cry of terror as the bear struck without mercy.

They reached the river to find that Alna and Vanu were already on board the ferry. Bolan and the nomads leaped on board and grabbed the ropes which propelled the craft across the river. Behind them the mayhem ensued as the bear pursued one slaver and then another, killing with claws and bone crunching jaws. It was in a frenzy, rushing hither and thither through the trees, trampling saplings beneath its feet as if they were but flowers. The slavers had dashed in all directions but the bear pursued them, catching each one, their screams heralding their deaths.

On the river Bolan and the others propelled the ferry towards the far bank. Halfway across the river the ferry came to a stop and was held in position by the system of ropes attached to oak piles on either bank which prevented it from being swept downstream in a strong current.

'Why have we stopped?' Alna asked, shivering with fear. 'Shouldn't we try and reach the safety of the other bank?'

'But we wouldn't be safe there,' Bolan said. 'If the bear pursued us across the river, we would be at its mercy on foot. So we must wait here. If the bear does pursue us then we'll cut the ropes and let the ferry drift downstream. It's our only hope of escape.'

At this they grew silent, listening to the bear as it marauded through the forest. But mercifully there were no more screams. Eventually the bear returned to the camp. It stopped well back from the fire and stood up on its hind legs to sniff the air. Dawn was just beginning to break and there was enough light with which to see.

The bear stood at the edge of the trees, a great monstrous creature seen in the grey light of dawn. A log collapsed in the fire, sending up a shower of sparks. The bear whimpered and drew back. It was afraid. But its fear was momentary. As its muzzle swung from side to side, sniffing the air, it roared its defiance.

With no enemy to challenge it, it dropped on all fours and lumbered along the edge of the camp, rising now and then to sniff the air. Suddenly it seemed to sense danger. It reared up and came at a run straight towards the ferry point on the river.

Bolan gripped Alna's and Vanu's shoulders, digging in with his fingers, warning them not to make a sound. There was no need to warn the nomads. They knew only too well the danger posed by the bear. From here they could smell it, a rank smell that was unmistakable. It was a smell that struck fear into man and animal alike.

The bear sniffed the air. But the wind was behind it and no scent carried to it from the ferry. And there was no sound either to alert it as the six persons on the ferry held their breaths. The bear dropped on all fours and sniffed the ground again, puzzled by the loss of the scent. Two or three times it stood up and then dropped down again.

During all this time the light was growing brighter.

The bear seemed to sense this now. It stared about, its great curved claws and white teeth clearly visible. It gave a last bellow of rage and anger, then turned about and, dropping down again on all fours, lumbered back towards the camp and into the forest. On the ferry they listened to its progress through the trees until the noise faded.

'You have done well, Bolan,' Kedo said. 'We are forever in your debt. Now we must eat. Then I will go and search for my father.'

'It's too dangerous,' Bolan said. 'He led Nevel and the slavers to the bear's den. If he was ...' Bolan hesitated, seeking a way of telling the nomad that Jode was almost certainly dead. 'If he didn't get away then he'll be near the den. It would be certain death to venture close.'

'We'll see,' Kedo said. 'But first we'll eat. There is plenty of food in the camp.'

Back at the camp they helped themselves to food, appetites returning after the first taste. When they had eaten, the nomads retrieved what they could from the camp and piled it together. Weapons and provisions, skins, clothing and various tools and cooking pots were gathered. As a people who relied on their own initiative for survival, nothing was wasted.

When this was done, Kedo went to search for his

father. Bolan tried to dissuade him but Kedo was determined to go.

'I'll come with you then,' Bolan said. 'After all, we owe Jode our very lives.'

Kedo nodded and they set off, following the path the bear had smashed through the forest. It had trampled everything underfoot in its rampage and in places they could see where its claws had torn branches from the trees when its progress had been impeded.

Deep in the forest they came upon the bodies of two slavers. Both men were dead and the sight of what the bear had done struck fear in both Kedo and Bolan. But after hesitating, they went on again. They were glad the wind was in their faces. At least no scent would be carried to the bear on the breeze. They moved cautiously, making no sound. If the bear were to get an inkling of their presence then they would end up like the slavers.

They began to climb, the ground becoming stony underfoot. It was then they came upon the body of another slaver, and 100 paces further on, they found Jode's body.

'We must cover the body,' Kedo said sadly, 'until we can retrieve it. We cannot leave it for the scavengers.'

Bolan helped to gather stones with which they covered Jode's body. As the last stones were laid in place, Bolan felt the salt prick of tears. Jode had given his life so they could live. He would never forget him.

Kedo stood for a moment by the pyre like a figure cut from stone. With bowed head he mourned his father. Then he roused himself and turned to face Bolan.

'Nevel and Bador must have died with the slavers,' he said. 'You have nothing to fear from them now. Come. We must return to the camp.'

They retraced their footsteps and as they passed the bodies of the two slavers they heard a groan from the undergrowth. Bolan and Kedo swung towards the sound, weapons at the ready. The groan came again, the unmistakable sound of a man in pain.

'One of them is still alive,' Kedo whispered. 'The bear mustn't have killed him.'

'It might be a trap,' Bolan warned.

Kedo nodded and took an axe from his belt. Gesturing to Bolan to be on his guard, the nomad crept cautiously into the undergrowth. After a moment he returned and beckoned to Bolan to follow him.

The injured man lay huddled on the ground. He was one of the slavers, the young leader Bolan had seen at the fire. His sheepskin coat, the finest garment Bolan had ever seen, was ripped from his shoulders. Clearly the bear had struck him a glancing blow, the claws tearing the coat, ripping the skin open to the bone.

The slaver stared up at them with pain-wracked eyes, his face devoid of colour from shock and loss of blood.

'Help me,' he groaned. 'Please help me.'

'Slavers.' Kedo spat out the word just as Jode once had.

'Please!' The young man's voice was weak. 'I'm not a slaver. My name's Olguin. My father is the Lord of Sarnay. He'll reward you if you help me.'

'Liar,' Kedo roared. 'You're one of slavers who've captured my people. You do not deserve to live.' With that he raised his axe.

As the stricken man cringed away from the blow that would kill him, Bolan caught the nomad's arm.

'Wait,' he warned. 'What if he's telling the truth? If he is, then the Lord of Sarnay might free your people in return for the safety of his son.'

Kedo hesitated. 'How do we know he's the son of the Lord of Sarnay?' he asked. 'Why would the Lord of Sarnay's son be with the slavers?'

'I speak the truth,' Olguin said. 'I wanted adventure. I slipped away from Sarnay with the slavers. If you bring me back, my father will give you whatever you wish. He will let your people go. Check my arm. On it you will find a tattoo. It will prove to you that I speak the truth.'

Kedo checked the young man's arm. On it, just above the elbow, was a tattoo of an eagle. It was the symbol of the Lord of Sarnay.

'You speak the truth,' Kedo said. 'We will help you in return for the freedom of my people. But you are seriously wounded. We must get you to the ferry and make haste to Sarnay.'

Kedo turned to Bolan. 'Go back to the camp,' he ordered, 'and get help. Quickly. There's no time to lose.'

Bolan nodded. He left the two men at a run, following the bear's trail to the river. With each gasping breath he was aware that if Olguin was not helped soon then he might die. If that happened the nomads were doomed. But it was not only the nomads who were in danger. Marn too could suffer.

If the Lord of Sarnay were to learn that what happened at the riverbank was responsible for his son's death, then he might destroy the village of Marn and take the people for slaves. Everything depended on Bolan and the nomads getting the injured Olguin back to Sarnay alive. If they did not then Jode may have died in vain.

11

ARRIVAL AT SARNAY

When Bolan reached the camp he explained briefly what had taken place, leaving no doubt as to the seriousness of the situation they were in.

'We must try and save Olguin's life,' he said. 'Otherwise the Lord of Sarnay will have revenge on us all.'

At this the nomads nodded gravely. But Alna and Vanu hung their heads and wept openly. The news of Jode's death hurt them deeply. They had both come to love the old nomad who had given up his life so they might have a chance to live.

Bolan felt helpless in the face of their grief. He tried to lift their spirits by telling them Bador was dead and that Nevel too was almost certainly dead.

But they were inconsolable and he left them to mourn in their own way.

For Bolan, there was no time to mourn. He would grieve for Jode later but now he had to get Olguin back to Sarnay. For safety's sake he moved Alna and Vanu off the trail and into the forest, leaving one nomad on guard. Accompanied by the other two nomads, he returned to where Olguin lay injured.

Kedo had tended to Olguin's injuries as best he could. The injured man was in great pain and had lost a lot of blood. Bolan realised that even carrying him to the camp might prove fatal yet they could not leave him here.

When the nomads lifted him up, Olguin fainted and mercifully remained unconscious all the way back to the camp. There Kedo and Bolan exchanged worried glances. Both were aware they could not take the injured man further. To do so would certainly kill him.

'We must seek help at Sarnay,' Kedo said. 'But a nomad can't go there. He would be taken for a slave immediately. They would not allow him to speak.'

'Then I must go,' Bolan said.

'It will be dangerous,' Kedo said. 'There are almost certainly other slavers scouring the countryside.'

'There will be danger,' Bolan said. 'But delay brings more danger for all of us. What if Olguin dies?'

Kedo nodded gravely. 'We have no choice,' he said. 'But you must not go alone.'

'Well, none of your people can join me,' Bolan pointed out. 'So I will take Alna. We will go together.'

'It is agreed then,' Kedo said. 'You must start at once. There is so little time.'

'I will speak with Olguin,' Bolan said. 'He can tell me who I should ask for at Sarnay. Meanwhile, prepare provisions for our journey.'

Bolan crossed to where the injured man lay by the fire. One of the nomads was tending the fire, heating stones which would be placed near the sick man to keep him warm. Olguin was becoming feverish and Bolan, who had seen many injured men, knew Olguin would soon become confused and lapse into unconsciousness. Bolan had little time left.

'I'm going to Sarnay for help,' Bolan said urgently. 'When I get there who should I ask for?'

'Ask for Varaka,' Olguin whispered, his face contorted with pain. 'He's my father's most trusted overseer. You must take this amulet with you and show it to Varaka. He will know then that you come from me.'

Bolan removed the amulet from about the man's neck. It was carved from bone in the shape of an eagle. The workmanship was delicate and intricate, and Bolan had never seen anything so fine before. He carefully concealed it in his tunic pocket. It was their insurance.

'I'll return with help,' Bolan declared, as he rose. He stared into the injured man's eyes and saw he was suffering a great deal. If he lived, then all would be well. But if not ...

Bolan now joined Alna who had already got their provisions ready. They would travel light, taking one pouch of food and one of water. Bolan slung his bow and quiver of arrows across his shoulder and checked the knife in his belt. They were ready for the journey.

They said goodbye to a very sad Vanu.

'I wish I was coming with you,' he said. 'I don't like being left alone.'

'We'll be back soon,' Bolan assured him. 'And while we're away our new friends will take care of you.'

Alna hugged Vanu and, with a tear in her eye, they left the camp. Kedo accompanied them to the ferry.

'I'll do what I can for Olguin,' he said. 'There are herbs and potions we know of which will help with the fever. We must hope now that the great spirits are with us.'

But as they reached the ferry it seemed as if the spirits had already deserted them, for the punt, which had been tied up beside the ferry, was on the other side of the river. It had been deliberately damaged.

'Nevel!' Bolan hissed the one word and Alna

gasped. 'Somehow he must have escaped the bear,' he added. 'He must have hidden in the forest until he had an opportunity to reach the river and cross it.'

'It could have been one of the slavers,' Kedo said hopefully.

'No!' Bolan was adamant. 'It was Nevel. I know it. A slaver might have risked the boat on the river. But Nevel wouldn't. Not after his ordeal. He has gone to Sarnay to tell the Lord that we killed his son.'

'Then we are doomed,' Kedo said. 'The Lord of Sarnay will send out his soldiers when he hears the news. They will not ask questions or listen but will kill everyone in the area. It's no longer safe for you to go to Sarnay. You must come with us and save yourselves.'

'No,' Bolan said quietly. 'We must go to Sarnay and tell the truth. Meanwhile, you must do all in your power to save Olguin's life. It's our only chance now. If he lives, then maybe the Lord of Sarnay will show us mercy.'

Kedo stared at Bolan. The young boy was a villager's son but he had the courage of a nomad. If he was willing to face the certain danger that awaited him at Sarnay, then they too must be brave.

'We will do as you ask,' Kedo said. 'Now go. And may the spirits be with you.'

Bolan nodded and he and Alna stepped onto the

ferry. Using the long poles, they propelled the craft across the river and leaped onto the bank. With a final wave to Kedo they turned their faces towards Sarnay.

They walked as fast as they could, knowing that to run would tire them out. They were already suffering from fatigue after the ordeal of the past days and nights but their sense of urgency kept them going. They were close to their goal now and must not fail. Even the possibility of the danger now awaiting did not slow their progress.

They had no thought for their surroundings, the forest which loomed up on either side of the trail or the open countryside it sometimes traversed. When the sun was high in the sky they stopped to eat, short of the hills they could see in the distance. Beyond those hills lay Sarnay.

After they had eaten they set off once more. Alna developed a blister on her left foot and Bolan had to tend to it. He rubbed some fat from the meat on the raw sore and then bound it with a strip of skin cut from his tunic. It gave Alna some small comfort as they pressed on. The trail led to the foothills and they began to climb towards the V that marked the cleft in the hills. They were exhausted when they reached the cleft and were able to look down on Sarnay and the blue expanse of the sea.

The sheer size of Sarnay took their breath away. It was at least 100 times the size of Marn, maybe even bigger. It was built on a finger of land that jutted out into the sea, cliffs dropping down on three sides so it could not be attacked from the water.

Bolan and Alna stared in awe at the settlement and the sea. Their grandfather had told them of the sea and the traders who came from Sarnay also spoke of it. Bolan and Alna had tried to imagine that great expanse of water, comparing it to the river at Marn, thinking it might be ten times wider than the river when it was in flood. But here the sea stretched in each direction as far as the eye could see.

Bolan then turned his attention to Sarnay itself. Across the finger of land, from sea edge to sea edge, a great rampart had been built of mud and stone. It was twenty feet high and at its bottom edge, giant oak spikes had been embedded. The spikes, set in serried ranks, pointed out and up at an angle, further strengthening the impregnability of the rampart. Three watch-towers commanded the rampart, one at either end by the sea's edge and one by the enormous oak gate which was the only break in the barrier.

Almost 1,000 paces back from the fortress were the flint mines. Here lay the original settlement of Sarnay. It had been built around the mines and was fortified by two massive palisades which made the palisade at Marn seem puny in comparison. Inside the palisades were the barracks, housing the soldiers who guarded the mines and the cages in which the slaves who worked the mines slept. There was a bakery, kitchens and the workshops where the craftsmen pressure flaked the flint to make scrapers, daggers, spears and arrowheads. Here too were the workshops of the craftsmen who fitted the handles to the implements, who made the arrows, who worked in leather and bone.

Bolan stared at the flint mines, aware that Jode's people were there. From his vantage point he could see the whole area and knew that no one could ever hope to escape from it. The nomads were doomed to live and die within the barriers if he could not persuade the Lord of Sarnay to give them their freedom.

A road ran from the flint mines to the fortress, joining the present road in a V some distance from the gate. Bolan ran his eye along its length until he came to the fortress itself. Within the ramparts, in the centre of the settlement, another palisade stood. Within its confines, the Lord of Sarnay had his quarters. Nevel was almost certainly there by now, telling his story. Soon they too would have to enter that area and confront the great Lord himself. Traders to Marn had often told tales of his cruelty and Bolan shuddered to think of them. What might he do to those he thought responsible for the death of his son? If they could not persuade him to believe their story then they would surely die or be sent to the mines.

'We must not delay,' Alna warned. 'Every moment counts. If Olguin dies before we get back to the river with help ...'

She let the threat hang in the air and Bolan shivered.

'We must go on down there,' Bolan agreed. 'As you say, we have no time to lose.'

He turned to look back the way they had come, aware that this might be their last chance to save themselves. But he could not run away; not now. Bravely he turned forward, facing Sarnay and whatever might await them there.

18

INSIDE THE FORTRESS

Bolan and Alna began their descent, uncertain of what might await them. The track was firm beneath their feet and they made good progress. They passed the flint mines on their right and reached the fork where the tracks merged. The one from the mines was constructed of wooden logs which had been hewn square and laid flat. It was obviously built for the easy transportation of goods and supplies between the mines and the fortress.

The timbers had been scorched to preserve then and were dark beneath their feet. They walked on, clearly visible to the men in the watch-towers who even now were probably sighting them along their arrows. Bolan glanced up at the watch-tower by the gate which was directly before them. He could see the soldiers and caught a glimpse of an arrow pointed through a slit in the massive oak beams from which the tower was constructed.

Bolan tensed himself, expecting an arrow to come hurtling towards him at any moment. But he realised this would not happen. Whoever was in charge of the watch-tower would wish to interrogate the two young strangers before taking any action.

As Bolan and Alna anxiously drew near the gate a smaller gate set in the main gate opened inwards and six soldiers emerged to block the way. They were dressed in leather and wore armour made of linked pieces of bone. They held spears at the ready before them. A seventh man now emerged and was clearly in charge. He too wore leather and bone armour.

He advanced to the head of the group, a large man with red hair.

'Who are you?' he demanded in a gruff voice.

'I'm Bolan,' Bolan said. 'This is my sister Alna. We are from Marn. My father, Gaelan, has come here to trade with the Lord of Sarnay.'

At this the soldier's eyes narrowed. Bolan saw him tighten his grip on his spear.

'Why have you come here?' he asked.

'We were on our way to meet our father,' Bolan

said. 'We came across a party of slavers from here who had been attacked by a bear.' Bolan decided not to tell the whole story. It would only complicate matters. 'One of the party is injured. His name is Olguin. He's the son of the Lord of Sarnay. He sent us to get help. He said we were to see a man called Varaka.'

'How do I know you are telling the truth?' the soldier asked.

'I have this,' Bolan said, putting his hand in his pocket to retrieve the amulet. But before he could withdraw his hand a soldier rushed forward and a spear point was thrust at Bolan's throat. Another soldier threatened Alna.

'Try to pull a dagger on us, would you?' the red-haired soldier asked. 'Well, we'll see what a spell in the flint mines will do for you.'

'We're telling the truth,' Alna insisted, stepping aside to avoid the spear that was pointed at her. 'The Lord's son is badly injured. He needs help immediately. There is no time to waste. If he should die and the Lord learns you delayed us, then you'll be sent to the mines.'

The red-haired soldier seemed to digest this information. He hesitated and Bolan saw his chance.

'I have proof that I speak the truth,' he said. 'I have brought an amulet from Olguin. It was that I was taking from my pocket and not a dagger. Olguin said I am to show the amulet to Varaka. Then he will know we speak the truth.'

'Let me see this amulet,' the red-haired man demanded.

Bolan withdrew the amulet and handed it over. The soldiers stared at it.

'That is the eagle of Sarnay,' one of the soldiers said. 'Only Olguin has such an amulet.'

'Why are you delaying then,' the red-haired man roared at Bolan and Alna. 'If the Lord's son should die then I will have to tell him you delayed in giving me the message. Come, come! I'll take you to Varaka. But leave your weapons here. None are allowed in the Lord's quarters except his most trusted bodyguards.'

He turned and hurried through the gate. Bolan gave his bow, arrows and dagger to a soldier and he and Alna followed. They crossed an open area which had barracks on either side for the soldiers. There were workshops here also where only the most skilled craftsmen worked. Also here were the living quarters of the most trusted slaves who worked within the fortress, and the buildings housing the bakery, granaries, storehouses and all the other facilities of a great settlement.

The soldier led them to the gate in the palisade. He rapped on the gate with the haft of his spear and a trap-door was slid across. This was only big enough for a man to peer out. A pair of eyes stared out at them suspiciously and the soldier stated the purpose of their errand. The amulet worked again. After a short delay the gate was opened and Bolan and Alna passed into the enclosed quarters.

They were taken by another soldier across a paved forecourt and into a large stone building. They found themselves in a bare room, a door from it leading to the depths of the building guarded by two soldiers. Even within his own quarters the Lord of Sarnay had to protect himself.

'Wait here,' the soldier ordered, and he disappeared through the door. The two men on guard watched them suspiciously. Bolan knew that at the least provocation the guards would kill them. Anxiously they waited and then heard footsteps on the stone floor beyond.

A man entered through the door. He was tall and well built, with dark hair and cold blue eyes. He wore a tunic which reached his knees, made of a material Bolan or Alna had never seen before. Below the knees he wore leggings of a similar material. The clothing was woollen and had been brought from countries across the sea where spinning and weaving were practised.

'I'm Varaka,' the man explained. 'You say you come from Olguin, that he is injured and needs help and he gave you this amulet which I have here?' His eyes were suspicious and angry.

Bolan nodded.

'He was attacked by a bear,' Bolan said. 'Alna and I found him. He is very ill and needs urgent attention.'

'Liar,' Varaka roared, and his voice echoed from the stone walls. 'Take them,' he ordered, and the two guards moved forward and held them at spear point. 'Olguin is dead,' Varaka said. 'He was killed by you and some nomads who escaped from a slaving party. We have learned all this from a man called Nevel who comes from Marn. He tried to save Olguin but you drove him away. We are now sending out a party of soldiers to bring back his body. When they return you and your father Gaelan, whom we trusted and helped, will be put to death. Then we will hunt down the nomads and they too will die.'

'It's not true,' Alna whimpered in fear. 'Olguin is alive. He needs your help, otherwise he will die. He gave us his amulet to prove to you that we speak the truth.'

'You stole this amulet,' Varaka went on, 'after you killed Olguin.'

'No.' Bolan shook his head. In his mind he sought words that might convince this man they spoke the truth. If they did not convince him then they would die and Nevel would live to return to Marn. 'Olguin gave me the amulet,' Bolan went on. 'He told me to ask for you. How could he have given me your name if he was already dead?'

Varaka's eyes narrowed. He frowned. Bolan saw his indecision and took his chance.

'Olguin is alive,' he continued. 'But he's seriously injured and will die if he doesn't get help soon. Let us go with the soldiers. We could not hope to escape. If we don't speak the truth, then the soldiers will bring us back here.'

'Why would we come here if we'd killed Olguin?' Alna added, as the man hesitated.

'Perhaps you are fools,' Varaka said. 'You might have thought we would give you a reward.'

'It's you who are the fool,' Alna said, her eyes now blazing with cold anger. 'While you stand here, Olguin is dying. You will not remain overseer for much longer if the Lord of Sarnay finds out that you ignored his son's cry for help. If we die, you'll certainly die with us.'

Varaka frowned again and his shoulders slumped forward. Their threat seemed to have unnerved him, just as it had unnerved the red-haired soldier. Varaka straightened up and the frown had left his face.

'Come,' he said. 'I'll take you to the Lord of Sarnay. Let him decide what should be done.'

19

THE LORD OF SARNAY

Bolan and Alna followed Varaka and found themselves in a long passageway lit by lamps hung high on
the walls. They had rush-pith wicks and were fuelled
by animal fat. The flickering flames threw weird and
grotesque shadows on to the floor.

Varaka led them on at a quick pace, their footsteps
echoing on the flagged floors. Many doors led off the
passageway. They were closed and the children could
only guess at what riches lay behind them.

Varaka turned into another passageway and here
they encountered two women who stood aside to
allow them pass by. The women kept their eyes fixed
on the floor. Bolan realised they were the personal
slaves of the Lord of Sarnay. They were the privileged

few who had escaped the mines but who would be sent back there at the least indiscretion.

At the end of the passageway an enormous oak door blocked further progress. Here two soldiers stood on guard, spears at the ready. But when they saw Varaka they lowered the spears and stared straight ahead.

Varaka opened the door and entered. Bolan and Alna followed him. They found themselves in a room as big as the whole Assembly House at Marn. It too was lit by rows of lamps mounted on the walls. The smell of the fat lay heavy on the air. The walls were draped with a fabric they had never seen before and there were bearskin rugs on the floor. In the centre of the room stood a massive oak table surrounded by intricately carved oak chairs. At the far end was another oak table and behind it another elaborately carved oak chair.

Directly behind the chair was a huge, empty fire-place. Above it a giant carved eagle hung on the wall. Bolan could not tell what it had been carved from but it certainly was not anything he had seen before. Varaka led them up to the table before the fireplace and told them to wait. Then he passed through another door on his right which was also guarded by two soldiers. Bolan and Alna waited, both trembling but desperately trying to hide their fear.

Varaka returned, followed by another man. He

was very tall and wore a black cloak which almost touched the floor. His dark hair was turning grey and his once handsome face was now lined and weather-beaten. Across his left cheek was a scar which ran from beneath his ear to his chin. He came forward and sat in the chair, the amulet held in his hands. He was examining it and frowning. Varaka stood beside him, his head bowed in deference.

The Lord of Sarnay looked up from the amulet and stared down at Bolan and Alna. His blue eyes were sharp and cold and his face seemed harsh and cruel in the dim light. His hands were clenched tightly about the amulet which was identical to the eagle which hung behind him.

'You bring news of my son,' the Lord of Sarnay said. His voice was soft but laced with menace. 'Tell me of him. Be brief.'

Bolan was weak from fatigue and fearful for all their lives. But he dredged up courage from a hidden source within himself and now spoke in a clear and commanding voice, repeating what he had already told Varaka.

'Liar!' The Lord of Sarnay brought his clenched fist down hard on the table. His face was suffused with both rage and sorrow. 'You dare tell me lies,' he shouted. 'I already know the truth. You have killed

Olguin and stolen his amulet. Nevel has told me the whole story. For that I will allow him to return to Marn and rule there. Your father, Gaelan, whom we trusted, is under arrest.'

'No.' It was Alma who whimpered.

But the Lord of Sarnay did not even notice this intrusion. 'The nomads would not help us,' he continued. 'They hate and fear us. They have helped you to kill my son. They will now be hunted down and put to death along with you and your father.'

'No!' Bolan was weak with fear but he held on grimly to the remnants of his courage. He stepped up to the edge of the table and spoke firmly. 'I bring you the truth,' he said. 'Your son is very ill. He will die if you do not help him. You must send whoever is most gifted at treating wounds to his aid. It's his only chance. The nomads help him because most of their people have been taken by your slavers. They want you to let them go in return for helping your son.'

Bolan stopped speaking and the room grew silent. The Lord of Sarnay closed his eyes and his knuckles showed white where he gripped the amulet. Eventually he opened his eyes and turned to his overseer.

'Varaka?' he said.

'It could be a trap, my Lord,' Varaka said. 'The nomads may have sent them to lure out your soldiers in order to kill them. They may seek revenge for having taken their people as slaves.'

'No.' Bolan spoke again. 'It is no trap. We speak the truth. We come here because we want your son to live. It is Nevel who has told you lies.'

'Very well.' The Lord of Sarnay held up his hand. 'We are sending our soldiers to the ferry. Arkan, our best man for treating wounds, will accompany them. You too will go with them.' He pointed his finger at Bolan. 'Your sister will remain here,' he added. 'If you speak the truth and my son lives then I'll grant you your freedom. If not, then you will die. That is all.'

'But my Lord ...' Bolan began.

'Silence!' Varaka's roar echoed in the room. 'You've heard the Lord of Sarnay speak. You must do his bidding.'

'Have this man Nevel arrested,' the Lord of Sarnay ordered. 'Hold him prisoner too until we hear news of Olguin.'

With that he rose slowly from his chair and left the room, his shoulders bowed as if under a great weight.

Bolan and Alna now followed Varaka from the Lord's quarters. Outside Alna was handed over to soldiers who were instructed to guard her with their lives. Varaka also ordered the soldiers to arrest Nevel. Now Bolan was handed over to Maklan who would lead the group to the ferry. Varaka ordered them to make haste. If they did not they would be sent to the mines on their return.

Bolan was exhausted and hungry. But he was as anxious as the soldiers to reach the river. Now that Alna and their father were prisoners it was imperative Olguin should live.

They set off after eating a quick meal of venison, the sun already dipping low on the horizon. They moved along at a rapid pace, Bolan in the centre of the group so he would have little chance of escape.

As they progressed, Bolan grew more and more exhausted. His mind began to wander and it took an effort to concentrate. But he kept on, thinking of the fate that would befall them if he failed. As darkness fell the soldiers lit torches and the march continued. By now Bolan was stumbling along among the men, his mind overcome with exhaustion. Somehow he managed to remain on his feet and as the moon climbed higher in the sky they reached the ferry.

Olguin had been moved into the ferry station. He was feverish but alive. At the news, Bolan collapsed on the ground and had to be helped to the shelter where Vanu slept. There Bolan threw himself down beside his brother and almost immediately fell into a deep sleep.

The sun was high in the sky when Bolan woke. He pulled aside the skin of the shelter and stared out, blinking in the glare. Maklan and Kedo were sitting together close to the blazing fire, which surely was not needed on such a hot day. Then Bolan realised the significance of the fire. Olguin must still be alive.

Refreshed by his sleep and by the realisation that Olguin still lived, Bolan rose. He was hungry both for food and information and crossed to where Kedo and Maklan sat.

'Olguin still lives,' Kedo told him. 'If he lasts this day and night then there is hope for him. The fever should soon break. We have sent a messenger to Sarnay with the news. Now you must eat.'

'Yes, eat,' Maklan insisted. 'You and the nomads here have done well. My master, the Lord of Sarnay, will reward you if his son lives.' With that he waved to one of the soldiers who was gambling close by. The soldier got up and brought Bolan a platter of food. Then Vanu, who had been playing at the edge of the camp, came running over to join his brother.

While he ate, Bolan told Vanu about the journey to Sarnay and about the settlement. He took care not to mention that their father and Alna were prisoners or that their lives were in danger. Vanu listened for a little while but soon got bored and went off to play again.

When Bolan had eaten he crossed to the shelter where the sick man was being tended by Arkan.

'I think he'll live,' Arkan told Bolan. 'He is young and strong and the nomad tended his wounds and cleaned them so there is not much infection.'

Bolan was satisfied. He was anxious for action of some kind yet there was nothing to do but wait. He joined the soldiers and heard stories of their adventures. As the day wore on, fatigue returned and after eating again, Bolan returned to the shelter to fall fast asleep.

It was dark when he woke but he knew when he looked out that it was close to dawn. Stars still prickled the sky with tiny holes of light and the moon was losing its glow. To the east there was a suffused light above the trees. Bolan got up and crossed to the shelter where Olguin lay. Kedo was there along with Arkan. Olguin was tossing and turning in his stupor and mumbling. Now and then he tried to rise and Kedo had to restrain him. Arkan was bathing the sick man's face, which glistened from sweat and water.

'The fever is at its highest,' Arkan said. 'By the dawn it will either break or he will die.'

Bolan waited with them as dawn turned the sky to a hazy pink which was soon burnt away by the sun. The soldiers woke and soon cooking smells were wafting in the morning air. Bolan joined the soldiers and as they ate other soldiers arrived from Sarnay.

They gathered around the fire and told of the Lord of Sarnay and his sorrow.

'He has made great promises to us all if his son lives,' they said. 'But we are destined for the mines if Olguin dies.'

The camp grew more solemn. They were all waiting now, their futures dependent on the sick man in the shelter. The sun rose higher and they sat in silence. Even Bolan was too fearful to go and enquire about Olguin.

They were all lost in their own thoughts when a shout went up from the shelter, taking them by surprise. Kedo emerged and whooped like a little boy.

'The fever's broken,' he shouted. 'Olguin will live. We are saved.'

20

NEVEL STRIKES

Bolan and two soldiers set off immediately for Sarnay with the good news. By now Bolan was fully recovered from his exhaustion and the realisation that Olguin would live gave him extra vigour. He bade goodbye to Vanu, assuring him that soon they would all be together again back at Marn. Kedo came with them to the ferry and told them that he and the others would shortly leave for Sarnay with the injured man.

Once on the trail they made rapid progress. The good news they brought with them seemed to give wings to their feet. It was close to evening when they reached the settlement. Over Sarnay there lay a deep gloom. Each person knew if Olguin died the Lord of Sarnay would be inconsolable with grief and they would all suffer his wrath.

Bolan and the two soldiers were admitted without question. Varaka was waiting for them inside the gate, his hawk-like face deeply worried. As the Lord of Sarnay's overseer, he would suffer most from his master's wrath. So it was with relief and joy that he heard the good news from Bolan.

'Come,' he said. 'You must convey this news to the Lord of Sarnay himself.'

Varaka led Bolan to the room where he had last seen the Lord of Sarnay. On that occasion Bolan and Alna had had to wait but now the Lord of Sarnay was already in the room. He did not sit on his chair but paced to and fro, his cloak billowing behind him.

As the door opened he swung about to face the callers, his features betraying his anxiety.

'We bring good news, my Lord,' Varaka said, bowing. 'Olguin is going to live. Bolan has brought us the good tidings himself.'

The Lord of Sarnay did not smile. But his features relaxed and his eyes brightened.

'It is good news you bring us, Bolan,' he said. 'You will be amply rewarded. Your father and sister will be released immediately. I shall also order the release of the nomads who were taken by the slavers.'

'Thank you, my Lord,' Bolan said, barely able to get

the words out. He could hardly believe his good luck. After so much adventure and misfortune, everything was working out fine in the end.

'See that this young man is fed,' the Lord of Sarnay said to Varaka. 'And bring his father and sister to his quarters. They may remain here for tonight. Release the nomads from the mines and ensure that the traitor Nevel is kept securely imprisoned. It will be for Gaelan to decide his fate.'

'Very good, my Lord,' Varaka said. 'I will see to it immediately.'

They were dismissed. Outside, Varaka led Bolan to a large room, divided into smaller sections by hanging skins.

'You may sleep here tonight,' Varaka said. 'I will arrange food for you, and have your father and sister brought here. Meanwhile, you may wash and I'll arrange a change of clothing.'

Bolan was fascinated by his surroundings. Beneath his feet was rush matting and the walls were hung with skins. When he drew aside one of the dividing skins he saw a raised wooden platform. It was spread with other skins and Bolan realised it was for sleeping on. He was tempted to lie down but decided he would wait.

Bolan walked to the window opening and drew aside the goatskin curtain. He found himself looking down on the courtyard of the Lord of Sarnay's quarters. He could see the gate in the palisade and he watched it, hoping to catch sight of his father and Alna.

The evening was drawing in. Shadows were lengthening and softening in the light of the setting sun. Out in the courtyard there was much activity as the slaves went about the last tasks of the day. Bolan was so engrossed in watching this that his father had already come through the gate and was crossing the courtyard before Bolan became aware of his presence.

Bolan knew immediately that something was wrong. His father, a tall well-built man, always walked with a sense of purpose. But his head was bent now as though he were anxious, his hand clasped to his shoulder. Bolan looked for Alna but there was no sign of her and a knot of fear tightened in his stomach. Surely nothing could have happened to her here? It was impossible.

Then Bolan's heart stumbled in its beat. Suppose a mistake had been made and she had been sent to the mines. Once his father went out of view, Bolan crossed to the door. He opened it and peered out, listening. He heard hurrying footsteps and then Varaka appeared, his father close behind him.

'What's wrong?' Bolan asked, his joy and relief at seeing his father dampened by his apprehension.

'Where's Alna?'

Varaka's thin face was creased with anxiety.

'Nevel has escaped,' he said. 'He has taken your sister as a hostage. He fooled the guards on the gate and they let them through. They left shortly after you arrived here with the good news concerning Olguin.'

'Father?' Bolan turned to Gaelan. Only then did Bolan see the blood on his father's shoulder, seeping between his fingers. His face was twisted with pain and he was breathing with difficulty. Bolan took a step forward. 'You're hurt.'

'It is nothing,' Gaelan said bravely, his teeth clenching with pain. 'A mere stab of a spear. I tried to stop Nevel ...' He shook his head. 'I'm sorry, Bolan,' he added. 'I've let you down. I've heard of all you've done. You've been so brave. But now you must be braver still and save Alna. I ... I can do nothing.' He swayed and a moan escaped his lips.

Bolan grabbed his father's arm and squeezed it.

'I will save Alna,' he said. 'And then Nevel will pay for his treachery.'

'The power of the Lord of Sarnay is at your disposal,' Varaka said. 'You have only to tell us what you want. I can have 100 soldiers ready to go with you at a moment's notice.'

'Thank you, Varaka,' Bolan said. 'But it is best if I

go alone. Nevel will try and get back to Marn and rally the men he still has in his power. Alna is his insurance. If he hears a great many soldiers in pursuit of him he may kill her and try to save his own life. Stealth is my only ally. So I will go alone. But I would be grateful for supplies and arms.'

'I'll see to it right away,' Varaka said. 'You can collect them by the main gate as you leave. I will send someone to tend to your father's wound. He should rest now.' With that Varaka hurried away.

Bolan and his father stared at each other. Then they embraced.

'Now,' Gaelan said, 'it is up to you. You are a brave son Bolan, and I know you will save your sister. Go now and may the spirits be with you. When you catch Nevel you must decide what his punishment will be.'

Bolan opened his mouth to speak. But there was a lump in his throat and he could not find words. Instead he embraced his father again and ran from the room. Gaelan staggered to one of the beds and sat down. In one week his son had become a man. He would make a fine leader when his time came, he thought. One day, under his rule, Marn might even become a great settlement like Sarnay.

21

CAPTURE

Outside, dusk was settling over Sarnay as Bolan picked up supplies of food, water and weapons at the main gate. As he left the safety of the fortress he heard the gate swing closed behind him and the heavy timber locking pieces drop into place. Bolan took one last look and then resolutely set his face towards the ferry.

He was convinced Nevel would keep to the trail and would make all haste to get back to Marn as quickly as possible. Bolan also assumed Nevel would expect a large party of soldiers from Sarnay to chase him. So when he saw no pursuit, it would lull him into a sense of false security.

Darkness came down quickly but Bolan kept

moving forward. He crossed the range of hills and saw a fire burning brightly in the distance. It was unlikely Nevel had stopped to eat but Bolan decided to take no chances and he approached the fire with caution. As he drew near he realised it was the camp of the nomads and soldiers who were returning to Sarnay with the injured Olguin.

Vanu was delighted to see Bolan. He wanted news of their father and sister and Bolan told his little brother that Gaelan and Alna were fine. He could not bring himself to tell the truth. He also told Vanu Nevel had escaped and that he was hunting him down.

Once Bolan had eaten Kedo drew him aside. He was aware something was wrong and Bolan told him the truth.

'I am sorry,' Kedo said. 'But we've seen no one.'

'Nevel would have seen your fire, just as I did,' Bolan explained. 'He might not have known whose fire it was but he would have taken care to avoid it. He has almost certainly slipped by in the darkness.

Kedo nodded. 'There's little you can do tonight,' he said. 'You must rest now. At dawn I'll come with you and we'll soon find your sister.'

'I cannot delay,' Bolan said. 'I must go on. I hate to think of Alna and how frightened she must be.'

'I understand,' Kedo said. 'But you cannot do

anything in the dark. If you go on alone you could be attacked by wolves. Wait until dawn and I'll come with you. I know you'll not mind me saying that I'm the best tracker of us all.'

Bolan nodded. 'I'll wait,' he said. 'But we must leave at dawn.'

'Rest now,' Kedo said. 'You'll need to be alert tomorrow.'

The camp settled down for the night. One soldier was left on guard. For a long time Bolan tossed and turned. But sleep eventually claimed him.

Bolan woke from a nightmare. He was trembling, his body soaked with sweat. The fire had burned down but in the moonlight he saw the guard.

Bolan knew he would not sleep again. He also knew he could not lie awake here all night. Alna could be in grave danger. By the time dawn came it may be too late.

Determined to act immediately, Bolan eased himself to his feet and picked up his bow, arrows and provisions. He did not want to rouse the camp or alert Kedo to the fact he was leaving. If Kedo became aware of his intentions, he would try to stop him.

Making hardly a sound, Bolan slipped out of the camp and took to the trail again. In the moonlight he made good progress, any fatigue forgotten in his anxiety for Alna's safety. On two occasions he heard wolves howling in the forest and he stopped to listen, his heart thumping audibly in his chest. On another occasion he heard the agonising screams of an animal close by and a rustling in the undergrowth as other creatures scampered away in terror.

He loped on as dawn broke and the darkness imperceptibly melted away. And it was then he saw the unripened blackberries on the ground. At first he thought they might have been blown down by the wind. But it was still too early for berries to be dislodged. And there had not been any wind to speak of. He kept watch as he walked along and noted the berries were to be found every few hundred paces. It was too much of a coincidence. Someone was deliberately picking and dropping them. Only one person would have thought to do that. It was Alna and she was marking the trail to let him know she had passed this way.

The realisation spurred Bolan on. He increased his speed but stayed alert for any sign of Nevel. He knew he would need the element of surprise on his side, for Nevel held all the advantages at present.

Bolan came upon Nevel and Alna quite quickly. He heard them up ahead, Nevel's anxious voice threatening Alna if she did not hurry. He heard her complain and then there was the sound of a blow and a cry echoed in the still morning. Bolan stiffened and fought the urge to rush blindly forward. What was needed now was guile.

'I must get ahead of him,' Bolan thought. 'It's my only chance. Nevel will not be expecting an attack from ahead. He'll be expecting danger from behind.'

His mind made up, Bolan left the trail and struck out into the forest. He wanted to get ahead of Nevel before he reached the ferry. Bolan decided he would have the best opportunity of taking Nevel by surprise there. And an idea of how he might do just that, hazy at first, but slowly gaining clarity was forming in his mind.

Giving the trail a wide berth, Bolan hurried through the trees. His anxiety urged him on and only when he was satisfied he had passed Nevel did he come back to the trail. He waited, concealed at the edge of the trail, until he heard Alna and Nevel approach. Only then did he run towards the river.

Bolan reached the river as the sun climbed in the sky, promising another warm day. Bolan climbed on board the ferry and removed the poles, which propelled the craft. He hid all but one of them in the trees. The remaining pole he left on the ground about 30 paces from the ferry itself. Then, he took shelter among the trees.

Nevel and Alna made good progress because shortly after Bolan settled in his hiding place he heard them approach. He peered out and saw that Alna's hands were bound in front of her. A rope was attached to her wrists with which Nevel dragged her along. She was clearly exhausted and stumbled along, weaving from side to side. Bolan felt a surge of anger but repressed it. This called for cool nerves. He could not allow his feelings to intrude.

Nevel dragged Alna to the riverbank and threw her on the ground. She posed no danger to him so he ignored her and boarded the ferry. When he realised the poles were missing Bolan could see him beginning to panic. He stared about, his head jerking here and there. Then he saw the pole lying on the ground and, leaping from the craft, he dropped his bow and arrows and scampered towards the pole.

Bolan emerged from his hiding place, an arrow notched in his bow. He stole forward until he was just behind Alna, who lay in a heap on the ground. Meanwhile, close by, Nevel was picking up the long pole.

'Nevel!' Bolan called out the name in a commanding voice so the other man froze.

'Bolan!' Alna roused herself at the sound of his voice and stared up at him in amazement. Bolan winked at her before he turned his attention to Nevel, who had swung about to face him.

Nevel's features were a mask of rage. He had almost succeeded in his escape and now, at the last moment, was being thwarted. His bow and arrows were too far away to be reached. All he possessed was his dagger.

'It's over,' Bolan said. 'You have failed.'

'Are you going to kill me?' Nevel asked in a frightened voice.

'I should kill you,' Bolan said. 'But I could not kill a man in cold blood. I'm going to give you a chance to gain your freedom. Come back and board the ferry. If you can get to the other side then you can go free.'

Nevel was so anxious to escape that he did not question the fact he was being given a chance of freedom. He picked up the pole, ran back and climbed on board the ferry. He began to propel the craft across the river, the anchoring ropes running smoothly in the grooves of the piles.

Bolan watched until he was halfway across. Only then did he call out to Nevel.

'Stop!' Bolan ordered, and Nevel ceased his efforts to look back. 'Throw the pole in the river,' Bolan ordered. He raised his bow and sighted the arrow on Nevel. 'Or I will kill you.'

Nevel hesitated and Bolan began to draw back the bowstring. With a curse, Nevel threw the pole into the river. The pole sank at first but then bobbed to the surface and floated away on the current.

'Here's your chance now,' Bolan said, his voice as

cold as an east wind. 'You can swim to the far bank. If you make it you can go free.'

Nevel stared back at Bolan, fear clearly visible on his face. The ferry, caught by the current, was straining at the anchoring ropes. Nevel, who had made their lives a misery, was now getting a taste of his own medicine.

'Swim to safety,' Bolan called out. 'Or wait until the soldiers from Sarnay come to take you to the mines. It's my sentence on you for your treachery.'

'Please,' Nevel begged. 'Please don't do this to me. I ... I cannot swim. Help me. I'll give you anything you want. I'll promise you anything.'

But Bolan was resolute in his determination not to succumb to Nevel's pleas. Too many people had suffered and died. He thought of Jode and Faver who had died due to Nevel's ambition to be headman of Marn. They had both been good men. Now Nevel's fate was in his own hands. He could show himself as a brave man or as a coward.

While Nevel begged for help Bolan cut Alna's bonds and told her all that had happened. He gave her food and water and they both sat in the shelter of the trees to wait for Kedo and the soldiers to arrive.

They came in the late morning. Kedo was relieved to learn that Alna was safe. The soldiers took Nevel from the ferry. Then they all turned for Sarnay, certain now that the great adventure was over at last.

22

A NEW BEGINNING

They reached Sarnay as darkness fell. A party of soldiers had been sent to meet them and it was a noisy group that arrived at the gate, torches lighting their way. While Nevel was taken to the mines, Kedo stood outside, unsure about entering Sarnay. No nomad had ever been inside the ramparts except as a slave.

Varaka came to welcome them and invited Kedo inside.

'Your people have been released from the mines,' Varaka told him. 'They are resting there in the soldiers' barracks. You may visit them whenever you wish. But first, we would like you to sample our hospitality. And the Lord of Sarnay himself wishes to thank you for helping to save his son's life.'

'I will gladly accept your hospitality,' Kedo said, smiling. 'But first I will go and see my people. I must reassure them they are safe.'

'Return here then,' Varaka said. 'Tomorrow you may leave us.'

Varaka turned to Bolan and Alna and asked them to follow him. He led them to the room in which Bolan had been reunited with his father. Here they found Vanu and Gaelan waiting for them. They had been anxious for news and now they knew that Bolan and Alna were safe, their relief was obvious. Gaelan's wound had been treated and though he was still weak from loss of blood, the colour had returned to his face.

Bolan and Alna had to recount their adventures for Vanu, who listened with wide-eyed astonishment.

'Soon it will be your turn to have such great adventures,' Gaelan told his son.

'But I've had great adventures,' Vanu said.

'Of course you have,' Gaelan said, and they all laughed.

Bolan and Alna washed and put on fresh clothing. They were then all taken into a great hall lit by lamps fuelled with beeswax. A long oak table with carved chairs stood in the centre of the flagged floor. Two logs fires burned at either end of the room and kept away any chill in the summer night.

Through an opening at the end of the room they could see into an adjoining room. Here, a gigantic wild boar was being roasted whole on a spit over an enormous fire. The smell of the cooking meat wafted through the room and reminded them that they were all hungry.

Kedo joined them, along with other important people from Sarnay. There was a giant blonde man who had come from across the seas. He wore wonderful clothes of many colours. About his neck hung an amulet in the shape of a wolf's head, intricately carved in amber.

The Lord of Sarnay entered and took his place at the head of the table. The other guests sat too and the great feast began. When all had eaten, dancers and singers performed for the guests. Then the Lord of Sarnay stood up and a silence fell on the room.

'We have gathered here,' he said, 'to celebrate the good news that my son Olguin is going to live. While out with a slaving party, he was attacked by a bear and left for dead in the forest. He would have died if three children from the village of Marn hadn't helped him.' At this the Lord of Sarnay pointed to where Bolan, Alna and Vanu sat. All eyes turned to them.

'The children were helped by some nomads who had been taken for slaves and had escaped,' the Lord continued. 'As a reward for their help, I have given them and the rest of their tribe their freedom.'

'But, my friends, the world is changing. More people are settling in villages. Still more come from across the sea, seeking new lands to grow crops, raise animals and rear their families. Soon the forests will disappear. So too will the bears and the wolves, the aurochs and the wild boar. There will be no animals left to hunt then and nomadic people will starve unless they adapt to a new way of life. Those who adapt will survive. Those who do not are doomed to extinction, like the animals.'

'You see here Kugor, who comes from a country across the sea.' The Lord of Sarnay indicated to the blonde giant. 'He brings news of new developments – of a material which can be used to make better blades and arrow and spear heads. Look at his clothes. They are made of wool. He tells us too that man has invented an implement which breaks up the soil. It is called a plough and can do the work of many men. It means we can cultivate more land. We can grow more crops and feed more people. With more people we'll have a greater demand for tools and clothing. With the plough more men will be free to work at crafts. Trade will increase and we will all prosper.'

He stopped to let his words sink in. 'With a greater number of people we will need more food. Gaelan, the headman of Marn village, is a wise man. He too has seen the world is changing. He came here to ask for this new wheat which gives a greater yield. I have made a decision that Marn will be the first village to be given this new grain. They will demonstrate to all others how a village may grow and prosper.'

At this, the children gazed triumphantly at their father. He smiled in return, pleased by the words of the Lord of Sarnay. Marn would not have to be split. Instead, as the Lord of Sarnay said, it would grow and prosper. By the time Bolan became headman, Marn would be the most important village under the protection of Sarnay.

'Think well on my words,' the Lord of Sarnay continued. 'Remember, we must change or perish. It is how we have survived for so long. That is all I have to say. Now let the celebrations continue!'

A great cheer went up from the assembled guests. The dancers and singers returned, performing late into the night. By then Vanu had crept onto his father's lap and had fallen asleep. When the party ended, Vanu was carried to bed. Kedo came with them to say goodbye. Tomorrow at dawn he would leave Sarnay with his people.

'Well,' Gaelan said, 'what do you think of what the Lord of Sarnay said tonight?'

'He speaks sense,' Kedo replied. 'I have known for

some time that our way of life is doomed. My father knew that too. I know he was relying on me to bring about the change that would save our people from extinction.'

'Will you settle down?' Bolan asked.

'We must,' Kedo said. 'We must settle or perish. Of course, there are many who oppose it. My task is to persuade them that my way is best. It will take time but eventually they will agree.'

'It must be done,' Gaelan said solemnly. 'And once you settle you will have the protection of Sarnay. The Lord of Sarnay wants to build a great trading empire. He wishes to import these new inventions from lands across the sea. Whoever is under his protection will prosper. There will no longer be the fear of your people being taken as slaves.'

'That's what I will tell my people,' Kedo said, nodding.

'It would be great if you were settled in a village,' Bolan added enthusiastically. 'We could help each other. We could visit you and you could visit us.'

'It's all like a dream,' Kedo said, shaking his head. 'But sometimes dreams come true. Even if we don't settle immediately, we'll remain friends. We'll call to you in Marn and maybe you'll come with us to hunt for wild boar. After all, I'll need someone to watch my back.'

At this they all laughed and after promising to visit, Kedo left to be with his own people. Bolan and Alna were still very excited by all the adventures and they sat talking with their father until they started yawning and Gaelan suggested they go to bed.

For a long time Bolan stayed awake, thinking of the exciting world that lay ahead. But eventually sleep claimed him and he dreamed of the future. In his dream he was headman of Marn, which was thriving and expanding under his leadership. They were preparing for a great feast. His friend Kedo was coming to visit. Kedo lived in a new village nearby and tomorrow they were going hunting together. Already the forest was dwindling, as more trees were cut down for farmland. The animals were disappearing too and Bolan hoped to hunt for wild boar.

'Soon there will be no boar left,' Kedo had said. 'So we'd best hunt them while we can.'

In his dream Bolan and Kedo were tracking a wild boar in the forest. It was the last one remaining in the area. At last they came on a clearing and there before them was the boar.

'It is yours, Bolan,' Kedo said and Bolan notched an arrow in his bow.

Bolan took careful aim but did not release the arrow. Slowly he lowered the bow and looked at

Kedo. There was an understanding in their eyes and Kedo nodded. They stood silently and watched the animal. After some time the boar stopped rooting in the ground. It trotted clumsily towards the trees and disappeared into the forest.

Bolan woke. It was almost dawn. He got out of bed and walked to the window, drawing aside the covering. From here he saw the sun rise. As he stood and watched the sun climb above the palisade, he felt he was at the beginning of a new and wonderful era. The age of stone was almost over.